Start Again

Ann Kingsdale

DEDICATION

To my parents. I love you.

ACKNOWLEDGMENTS

To my beta readers Erin, Colleen, and Leigh Anne. I appreciate your kind words and feedback. To Adam Schmitz, who kept me going on this writing journey. Thank you for all your encouragement and support, I am eternally grateful.

CHAPTER 1

The wheels clanged and shuddered when they touched the ground and the plane lurched as it began its fast decent down the tarmac. Rena's stomach twisted into knots. Taking off and landing was not something she enjoyed, and considering she hadn't flown in ten years, this was not something she had remembered fondly. *Ugh.* She breathed a sigh of relief when the plane started to slow down. "Finally," she thought, her apprehension somewhat waning. *I am finally here, on solid ground.* Not that the plane ride had been all that terrible. It had been mostly smooth, with one hour of turbulence that hadn't really been all that bad. But this was all new to her. She hadn't been outside of the country in years. She hadn't been anywhere in years.

"Welcome to Rome," the pilots voice interrupted her thoughts. "We hope you enjoy your time in the city of love."

The plane exploded with a thunderous clap of applause from the passengers. "At least someone is enthusiastic," she thought.

Rena looked out of the window while the plane starting taxiing along the tarmac to the gate. It had been hard enough for her to even get on the plane, and now she wasn't sure she could even get the courage to get off it. Her apprehension started to rise again. "I'm not sure this was a good idea," she thought. She had finally given in to Anna a month ago after constant pressure for her to come and visit. Anna had been her best friend in university. They had met each other the first day they had both started as freshman, and Rena had known they would be friends for life. They were as different in personality as they were in looks. Anna was an enthusiastic, wild and crazy extrovert, with jet-black hair and dark brown eyes, while Rena was more of a calm, introspective soul with blonde hair and blue eyes. Their contrasting looks and personalities made them quite the spectacle to look at on the university campus, and many of their classmates had wondered how the two of them could be friends. But deep down, both knew from the start that they were soul sisters.

"Rena you've got to live again!" Anna had said on the phone. "Come to Italy and stay with me, it will be perfect!" Anna rolled her 'r's in the word 'perfect' for dramatic effect.

"She has always been a drama queen," Rena thought with fondness for her friend dramatics. But Anna had continued to use her charms and had not really given Rena a choice.

"You have to come here Rena; I will be so bored and lonely here all alone. What will I do with myself? C'mon Rena, we can have fun, like old times! I need you here," Anna had pleaded.

Anna's husband Simon was a restaurant mogul with a strong following and frequently accepted invitations to cook and teach all over the world in North America, Europe, Asia, and the Middle East. Anna usually travelled with him, but on occasion, when she felt like it, enjoyed staying in Italy, in the town of Ariano Irpino, which they considered their home base. This time Simon was invited back to Saudi Arabia for a culinary teaching tour and Anna did not want to go. "I've been there already Rena, same old same old. I would rather hang at the beach with you and chat about old times." Anna sounded so desperate that Rena couldn't help but laugh, and finally gave in. She knew Anna's heart was in the right place, and that she was worried that Rena wasn't moving on from her husband's death.

Rena hadn't moved on the way Anna would have wanted. She hadn't travelled, worked, been out much, or been good at keeping in contact with most people. But Rena didn't really feel like she needed to get away. Since university, Anna and Rena had stayed in touch, and they had shared most things, their dating lives, engagements, weddings and work life. "But not everything," Rena thought. Not what happened after the wedding, Rena had not shared that. If she was honest with herself, she had felt like she had got away already since Jarod had died. The marriage hadn't been easy on Rena. It had been tough, lonely, and had taken part of her soul. When Jarod had first died, she was devastated, he was her husband and she had loved him. But later, a part of her, a part deep inside her, had felt the shackles of her soul break free, and she had felt relieved. But she couldn't tell anyone that. Everybody had loved Jarod. He had always been the life of the party, the one everyone was drawn to, the one everyone admired. She sighed inwardly to herself. "Nobody can ever know how I really feel," she thought. She only hoped she could keep it from Anna.

Rena waited until most of the passengers left the plane and then stood up and got her carryon bag from the

3

overhead compartment. There were only a few passengers in front of her and she walked quickly down the aisle and smiled at the pilot who was greeting the passengers as they left the plane. She followed the other passengers through the crowds to customs, and after a brief wait, handed the customs agent her passport and waited patiently while it was reviewed and stamped. She retrieved her passport and then looked around for some familiar faces from the plane and found the carousel where she had to get her bags. She waited with the rest of the passengers from her plane and noticed several of them looking out through a glass wall, excitedly pointing and waving at friends and family waiting in the arrivals lounge. Rena stretched her neck and peered through the glass to see if Anna was anywhere to be seen. "It will be great to see Anna again," Rena thought.

Excited cries erupted behind her and Rena saw the luggage begin to tumble out onto the moving carousel. Rena waited for few minutes and then spied her bags and leaned in between other passengers and picked them up from the carousel. "Here we go," she thought as she put the luggage on the ground and proceeded to wheel her bags toward the exit doors beside the glass wall. An elderly couple walked slowly ahead of her through the doors.

"Zio, Zia, boujournio. Cosi bellovederti!," Rena heard as the automatic doors were opened.

A couple with three children just outside the doors ran towards the elderly couple showering them with kisses. Rena struggled with her bags to get by them, and eventually got through.

She looked around. The airport terminal was crowded and loud with lots of yelling and kissing. Rena had never been in such a loud arrivals lounge or had ever seen so much kissing going on. Everywhere people were holding

4

up cheeks to be kissed. "Italians sure love to kiss," she thought. She looked at all the faces waiting in the arrivals lounge and tried to find Anna. Where was she? This was typical Anna. Always late. Anna lived by a time clock like no other. In university Rena was surprised that Anna had always looked so well put together considering she always slept in and never got anywhere on time. *Where is she?* Rena looked around and her eyes were drawn to an older man standing in a corner, away from the crowd. He was staring at her intently. He was short and stout and looked like a big round teddy bear. He looked directly at her, and then down at a picture in his hand and let out a big toothy grin. "Rena, bella, bella," he said enthusiastically as he approached her.

"Anna, I'm going to kill you," thought Rena.

The man approached her with outstretched arms and Rena had a moment of panic before her worse fears were realized. "Bella, bourjourno," the man said as Rena's face was grasped in two chubby hands and two big kisses were promptly bestowed on each cheek.

"Anna you are going to die," decided Rena inwardly.

The man let go and held her at arm's length. "You are so, bellisima, what you say, pretty?" he said in broken English. "My Anna tell me much about you." I'm Zio Augusto." He paused. "Uncle Augusto, yes?" he said sounding pleased with himself.

"Was that a question?" thought Rena.

He looked intently at her. "I guess he is expecting an answer," she thought. "Zio Augusto" she said nodding and gave him a shy smile. Zio Augusto beamed.

"Come, come, venire," he said grabbing her bags and gesturing towards the doors to the car park. Rena followed

Zio Augusto through the crowds to the car park and a small Fiat. Zio Augusto put one bag in the trunk and one in the back seat and gestured to the passenger seat. "Si, Si" he gestured opening the door. Rena got in.

***

If Rena had thought the hour of turbulence on the plane was bad, nothing had prepared her for the drive with Zio Augusto. Zio Augusto sped along the winding roads to Ariano Irpino only slowing down sporadically to yell excitedly and shake his fist at other cars that he passed on the way. Zio Augusto spoke continuously in a mix of Italian and English but Rena barely noticed. She nodded occasionally to what Zio Augusto was saying, and gripped the armrest of the door hoping that she would make it to see Anna in one piece. She had heard about the driving in Italy, but had thought it was a joke.

After one hour, she realized that nothing was going to entice Zio Augusto to slow down, and gathered a bit more courage and started to look outside the car at the countryside around them. She had to admit that the scenery was beautiful along the road to the province of Avellino. The road wound along the bottom of beautiful mountains that were tall, green and majestic with grey peaks that poked out the tops. Rena saw small towns nestled in valleys and sprawling villas built into the mountainsides. "The views from their windows must be spectacular," she thought. Fields of yellow, purple and white flowers speckled along the roadside and Rena soaked in the wonderful scents that floated on the breeze into the car. "No wonder Anna wants to live here," Rena thought. She hadn't known Italy could be so beautiful. The scenery was breathtaking, and the beauty of it all reminded her of the countryside at home. *Home.* Her thoughts drifted to what she had left behind. She had felt stifled. The breeze coming into the car made Rena relax. "Anna is right," she thought. "This is a new start. Time for me to be free, and enjoy life," she thought.   She knew she deserved it.   It had been a long time coming...

CHAPTER 2

It hurt. It hurt when he ignored her. It hurt when he never asked her what she liked, what she loved, how she felt. It hurt when he would not look at her. It hurt that it took an effort for him to respond to her. It was years of hurt. She was worth more. She deserved more than the love he gave. More than the love he was capable of giving. She craved more... and the more she craved...the more it hurt. And now he was gone. She felt free, relieved, and she felt guilty. But she shouldn't...

Rena woke up with a start. She quickly looked around and then sighed and fell back into the freshly laundered sheets. She had arrived in Ariano Irpino last night with Anna's Zio Augusto. The four-hour trip from Rome had been stimulating to her senses, and Rena had not wanted to miss one view, but the flight and drive had been tiring and Rena had barely looked at her surroundings when she had arrived at Anna's home. She had noticed the home looked white and grand and had a red door. "Only Anna would add a red door to a white house," Rena had thought chuckling. Rena had quietly followed Zio Augusto to the door. Anna had opened the door right away and greeted them quickly having one look at Rena and promptly sending her to bed. Rena barely remembered climbing up the stairs to the guest room. The bed had looked so inviting that Rena tumbled into it quickly.

She stretched her arms and lay back on the pillow. She was not sure how long she had slept, but she felt good. "It is nice to be somewhere different," she thought. Rena looked at her phone and noticed it was almost 5 am in Toronto. She didn't want to stay in bed all day, so she gingerly stuck a toe out of the bed and moved herself to a sitting position. Her toe touched the floor and she expected a cold feel, but it was warm to the touch. She looked around the room. Marble flooring covered the floors and the walls were painted a metallic gold with flowing creamy white curtains. "Anna has great taste," thought Rena. She climbed out of the bed and slowly moved to her suitcase that was sitting on a mahogany armchair and rummaged through it for some clothing. "A sweat shirt and sweat pants will do for now," she decided. She got dressed and then went into the adjoining bathroom to pull a quick brush through her hair and quickly brush her teeth. "Now I must go and find Anna," she thought.

Rena walked to the landing outside her room. Floors of marble and a beautiful ceramic staircase greeted her. The house was big, beautifully decorated and Rena felt like she had stepped into a palace. Artwork adorned all the walls on the landing, and small glass and marble tables were situated outside each room with vases of fresh flowers. She hadn't noticed much about the house the night before, but looking around she thought it was beautiful. "Anna you have such great taste," Rena thought again.

She got to the head of the stairs and tiptoed down. She wasn't sure what time it was in Italy, but the sun was shining through the beautiful window above the front door at the end of staircase. She smelled something delicious baking, and her stomach growled in response. It had been several hours since she had last eaten on the plane. She turned left at the bottom of the staircase and moved down the hallway toward the smell. The walls on the bottom floor were adorned with renaissance looking paintings and marble tables with jeweled vases and pink and violet roses. She moved toward the smell of the baked goods and entered into a big spacious kitchen.

The kitchen was long and wide, and almost as big as Rena's apartment in Toronto. The cupboards were a white linen colour. Beneath them was a white granite counter holding glass jars of various types of pasta, rice and beans. A huge wooden table sat center in the kitchen. Rena turned to the sound of clanging and noticed Anna working beside the stove. Her raven-coloured hair was pinned on top of her head, and she was wearing a pink apron, busily mixing something. The radio was on with a catchy tune and Anna was dancing to the beat while she furiously mixed something in a bowl.

"Well, I never expected to see this! Italy has domesticated you!" Rena said loudly. Anna spun around with a huge grin on her face.

"Rena, you're awake!" she cried, dropping the bowl heavily on the counter and running to hug Rena with outstretched floury arms. Rena hugged her tightly and Anna sped her around until Rena felt dizzy. She held her in outstretched arms. "A little skinny you are, and a bit pale, some good food and sun will get you healthy in no time," Anna said grinning at her. Rena laughed. Anna had always been the mother hen in university. She had been aptly named the "mother hen" in their college dorm, as she was always looking out for their friends. But even though she had been called the mother hen, she had still been a partier.

"She was always the life of the party," thought Rena reminiscing. Hugging Anna felt like coming home. "It's great to be here," said Rena.

"Good," said Anna and smiled devilishly, "because I have a lot of plans for you."

CHAPTER 3

Anna's white Fiat sped along the road. Rena looked out the window and enjoyed the beautiful view. It had been two weeks since she had arrived in Italy and she already felt like a new person. She and Anna had reminisced together, and enjoyed many days of walking, eating, and chatting. It was therapeutic and Rena was starting to feel like a great burden was lifting. She felt lighter, and free. It was a long time since she had felt this way. "It's amazing how breathtaking Italy is," she thought as Anna's Fiat sped along the winding roads. The road up the mountains to Bicarri was very twisty with turns of 180 degrees and sometimes 360! Rena's stomach reacted at first, but the scenery had awed and distracted her and eventually she didn't notice the effect on her stomach. Quaint villages and beautiful fields with bright yellow flowers, and the smell of oleanders and poppies dominated her senses.

Earlier in the day, she and Anna had enjoyed a terrific breakfast with melt in your mouth homemade biscuits, fresh ricotta cheese and tomato from the garden. "Let's go to Bicarri today to see Falcone," Anna said mischievously between mouthfuls. Rena almost choked on her food.

Anna laughed. "Maybe Falcone is right," she said, "You *must* think he is a god to choke like that!" Rena laughed. Falcone was Anna's cousin, and Rena had met him in Toronto many times. To say that he was an outgoing guy was a huge understatement and did not do him justice. Falcone was what one would call a real life Ricco Suave. He had it all going for him, the dark looks, great muscular body, and women throwing themselves at him. And he threw himself in their direction as well. Rena recalled many times where Falcone decided she was his next conquest, and surprised her with a quick pinch on her bottom, and once even a long deep kiss.

"I know you love me, "Falcone would say. " You are just shy." That didn't stop when Rena married Jarod either. Falcone did not care; all women were available to him. He loved women. And Rena loved him. As a friend. He made her laugh, and it felt good to have someone pay attention to her.

"What's he doing here in Italy?" Rena asked.

"He's here on a police exchange or something," Anna said. I told him you were coming and he made me promise to bring you for a visit," she said rolling her 'r's when she said 'promise'. "I hope you have your chap stick handy," she said giggling.

Rena laughed. "Maybe I will put some on now," she said smiling and reached into her purse.

***

He hadn't looked at her all day. Not once. She asked him to rub her shoulders. They were sore and tense. He would not touch her. He said he would rather rub something else and indicated the space between her legs. She told him that she loved having her shoulders rubbed. He said he didn't like to do that, but he would rub the space between her legs....That was the only time he looked at her.

The trip to Bicarri took one and half-hours. Rena and Anna chatted about old times, old friends and college days. It was great to be in her company again. Once in Bicarri Anna parked the Fiat in a car park and her and Rena walked to the piazza to meet Falcone. The piazza was bustling with people attending a market. The piazza had white cobble stone roads, and was lined with trees and quaint old buildings. Anna gestured Rena towards a semicircle of marble stadium seating on the outer edge of the market. Rena climbed up the marble steps to the top and sat down on the cold stone. She looked around. It was breathtakingly beautiful to sit on the stone and watch the activity below. "We'll wait for Falcone," Anna said plunking herself beside her. "Although, I am sure he will find *you*," she laughed.

"You're probably right," laughed Rena. "He always seems to." They both laughed.

Rena relaxed and closed her eyes with her head turned to the sun. The brightness and warmth of the sun was like a comforting blanket that contrasted with the cold marble she sat on. She breathed in, relaxing even more and enjoying the sounds of the market below. As she breathed in again, she felt hot breath in front of her face. She opened her eyes and made a little squeal. Leaning over her with a big grin on his face was Falcone.

"Ciao bella," he drawled seductively and leaned forward. Rena giggled and pushed him out the way.

"Good to see you Falcone, I see you haven't changed," she said.

"Not when it comes to beautiful women," he said, leaning forward again and planting a kiss on each of her cheeks.

"Geeze, what about me?" asked Anna pretending to be jealous.

"Kisses for you too cousin," Falcone said as he greeted Anna the same way.

"Falcone looks great as usual and he knows it," Rena thought smiling. He had the same dark hair and dark Italian colouring like Anna, and if you didn't know they were cousins, they could easily be mistaken as twins. Falcone smiled at the girls with his usual mischievous grin.

"So, are we going to just sit here or go get a coffee?" he laughed and jumped down the steps. Rena and Anna got up and followed him.

They walked to a nearby café on the other side of the piazza where they sat at a small round table on a patio. Falcone ordered espresso with Sambuca and almond and lemon biscotti. The café had many tables and was crowded with patrons talking excitedly in Italian and using their hands for emphasis. Rena, Anna, and Falcone chatted a bit about Falcone's work in Italy. He and a team of others from Toronto were in Italy to learn about some of the workings of different police forces to see if they could use some of the information in their policing in Toronto, and to share some of the tools the Toronto Police force used as well. It was interesting and Rena asked him a lot of questions about what they were learning and what they hoped to accomplish.

"Lots of questions sexy, but seriously we don't need to talk" Falcone said slyly winking at Rena and grabbing her hand.

"Oh man!" said Anna, "you just don't give up."

Falcone laughed, "Never" he said grinning and kissed Rena's hand passionately. Rena laughed. It was good to be in his company again, and although she didn't feel attracted towards him in that way, it was great for her ego.

Falcone's phone rang and he excused himself from the table and went to the piazza to take the call. Anna looked at Rena.

"You know Rena, Falcone is not all that bad. I think you two would make a good couple."

"Oh, Anna," Rena said. "I don't think of him in that way. I mean, he is great looking, okay fantastic looking, and very charming, but he is not my type," she said truthfully.

"Was Jarod?" Anna said looking at her meaningfully. Before Rena could react, Falcone came back throwing money on the table.

"Come on bellas, we are going to go and meet the guys and have some fun," he said.

"Really?" said Anna, "What are we going to do?"

"It's a surprise cousin, but you will love it," he said grinning.

CHAPTER 4

They drove from Bicarri towards Laco Pescara following Falcone's red Fiat. "Do you know where we are going?" Rena asked Anna.

"Ha! No idea, who knows with Falcone," Anna said concentrating on the road. "But we are driving toward the lake, so maybe a nature walk?" she suggested.

"Oh, that sounds great," said Rena. "The mountains here are so beautiful. A nature walk will be amazing," she said enthusiastically. Anna's car followed Falcone's Fiat into a driveway with a sign for Albero Avventura.

"Ha-ha," laughed Anna. "Looks like we are going to be doing some tree walking!"

"Tree walking?" Rena asked.

"Yes, you walk high up on ropes in the trees. The views are very beautiful, you will love it," Anna said with enthusiasm.

Rena looked down the drive at the tall trees. Her heart

17

sank a little bit. She wasn't keen on heights. She shook it off. "This is an adventure, my time to try something new. It can't be that bad," she thought. *I can do this.*

Anna parked her white Fiat beside Falcone's car. Falcone was already out of his car huddling with a group of men a few spaces away. Anna glanced at Rena. "Those guys look buff," Anna said slyly.

"Yah, not bad at all," said Rena admiring the men from afar. There were about ten of them standing around and laughing. All of them looked tall, muscular and tanned; like a bevy of Greek gods. "This is going to be fun," Rena said smiling.

"Yes, well you need fun," said Anna grinning. "But don't take any of them seriously, they are Falcone's work mates and we all know the reputation police have," she warned.

"Yes," said Rena chuckling, "but I will enjoy the view."

The girls got out of Anna's Fiat and marched up to the men. As they marched closer, the men looked less like Greek gods, and more like a group of ordinary guys out to have some fun. They were all dressed in athletic wear and matching T-shirts. One of the group called out to Anna. "Hey Anna, so good to see you," he cried. He marched away from the group and greeted Anna with a kiss on each cheek. He was tall and appeared to be a bit older than the rest of the group, his temples showing the first shades of grey.

"Hi Matt," said Anna giving him a quick hug. "I didn't know you were here."

"Yes, got away from Martha and the kids for few weeks," he joked.

"You must miss them," Anna said.

"Definitely" said Matt, "But the girls are a bit older now, so easier for me to get away." He looked at Rena and smiled. His smile was warm and inviting. Rena liked him almost immediately. Anna was about to introduce him to Rena when Falcone turned around.

"Hey guys," he said, nodding to the group. "This is my cousin Anna and her good friend Rena." The men turned around and looked at them.

Rena looked at the men and smiled. They all seemed like nice, confident men. "Well, most cops are," she thought. Falcone called to the other side of the parking lot.

"Hey Carl, hurry up," he yelled.

From far Rena saw a man running up. "He looks like another Greek god from far away," thought Rena. As the man approached, the other men greeted him, patting him on the back and joking with him.

"Took you long enough buddy." The man smiled.

Rena felt a flutter in her stomach. The man's smile was similar to Matt's but had a totally different effect on her. He was a younger version of Matt, tall, muscular, medium build and athletic looking. He was wearing the same attire as the other men but his clothing seemed to fit that much better. He pulled off a baseball cap. Sandy brown hair tousled out. The man turned from his buddies to look at her and Anna. Falcone gestured to him.

"Anna, Rena, my buddy Carl," "Carl, my cousin Anna and her friend Rena," he said. "Be easy on Carl today," Falcone said, "he had a rough night." The other men laughed.

Carl smiled at Anna, moved forward, and shook her hand. "Poor girl, must be difficult having a cousin like

Falcone, I bet he is always hitting on your friends."

Anna laughed. "Ah yah, and this one especially," she said looking at Rena.

Carl turned to look at Rena. He smiled and held out his hand. "Oh my god," thought Rena, "that smile." Rena took his hand. A wave of electricity went through her. Her hand burned with his touch. *My god, he has the brownest eyes I have ever seen.* They were the colour of dark molten lava and melted into her, like deep pools of nothingness. She could be lost in them. *And that smile.* It was big, inviting, *really inviting.* Rena smiled and shook his hand. She hadn't had this reaction to a man in such a long time, or any time for that matter. *Maybe I've had too much sun.*

***

Carl couldn't stop staring at her. He was surprised Falcone had never mentioned her. "Probably keeping her to himself," he thought. She was beautiful. Her big round blue eyes held his intently. Holding her hand, he felt like he had seen her somewhere before, met her before. But he knew he hadn't. He wouldn't have forgotten this. She was shorter than he was, and looked a little impish. Her eyes were framed by a long face and shimmering blond hair. Her smile lit up her face, and her eyes twinkled. Carl felt his body react to her smile. "This can only lead to trouble," he thought.

It had been years since Carl had had a reaction like this to a woman. Sure, he had his fair share of woman over the years, and had made sure he did. Heck, he enjoyed women. He wasn't going to lie. They smelled good, were usually good company and he enjoyed romping around with them. It was safe. Woman weren't to be trusted. Carl had learned that the hard way. His first marriage had been a disaster. He had been busy training to be a cop, while

Amber was working through law school. They lived crazy separate lives at that time, getting together for sex and a few moments in between. Once they both graduated, Amber had been insistent on starting a family. Carl wasn't sure if he was ready for it, but decided it was worth the *practice*. Then the worst happened. Carl went for a routine physical checkup at work. He had been tired and had noticed a bump on his neck. But he was a healthy guy and had thought nothing of it. But the routine checkup had uncovered Hodgkin's Lymphoma. The next couple of years he had undergone treatment, chemotherapy and radiation that wiped him out and sometimes made him so sick he couldn't see. Amber had stayed through it all, but Carl knew deep down that it had been hard on her. Once he had finished treatment, they tried to have children again, but nothing happened. They both were tested and it turned out Carl could not have children. After that, the marriage broke down and Amber left. Carl was left shattered, but he had pulled himself together, rebuilt his strength and his health and moved on. He had vowed, to never fall in love again. And then he had.

This time it was Joanne. He had met her during police training camp and knew her well. Things just seemed to sync and he thought that this was how things were meant to be in the first place. Somehow, everything made sense. That was until Joanne came home claiming that she was pregnant. He had been so excited, so elated that they were having a child. But eventually he heard rumours. Rumours about Joanne and other guys on the force. His brother convinced him to be tested again. The doctors broke the news to him that he was still infertile. There was no way the child Joanne was carrying was his. Shattered again, Carl vowed that he would never fall in love again. And he had never felt anything for any other woman he had met since. Sure, he had liked a lot of them, but nobody had taken his heart. It was his alone.

This woman in front of him had surprised him. He watched her closely as the group walked up the path to the ticket booth. She was chatting away with his brother as if he was an old friend. He couldn't stop staring at her and shook his head a few times to stop himself. "Why am I so attracted to her?" he wondered. He couldn't figure it out. Yes, she was beautiful, but he had had beautiful before. He considered himself a good-looking guy and could get any woman he wanted. He didn't need fixate on anyone. But there was something about her. *Something in her eyes.* He couldn't put his finger on it...

CHAPTER 5

He was fixing the garage opener. He asked her to climb the ladder and pull the opener cord. He started to close the garage door. She felt panicked since she was claustrophobic. He got annoyed with her and told her it was fine, they could get out. He told her to climb the ladder. He knew she was afraid of heights. She had told him. He sighed and got annoyed as she climbed up. He told her she was taking too long. She felt sick to her stomach. She told him she was going as fast as she could. She finally got up and he asked her to pull the garage opener cord. She had to reach from the ladder. She panicked and told him she was not sure she could do it. He got frustrated with her and told her to get down. He was angry.

Rena could feel his eyes boring into her back. They were getting connected to safety harnesses to begin their tree trekking. After they had bought their tickets, the group had been assembled in a small building where they had listened to a briefing of the rules. After all of the rules had been explained, each of them had signed a long waiver, and were now ready to ascend into the trees. All the while, Rena could not help but notice him. He was muscular, lean, and strong, and his muscles seemed to ripple every time he moved. And that smile... "What's wrong with me?" thought Rena.   She had turned away from him to stop this nonsense. But now she could feel him looking at her.

"Com'on Rena," Anna said breaking the spell, and grabbing her arm and handing her a helmet. "Let's get going, I'm so excited." Rena was happy for the interruption of her thoughts and quickly followed Anna to the start of the trek.

Rena looked up at the ladder on the tree, and saw the bridge at the top at the beginning of the trek. "The route doesn't look that bad, and isn't too high," she thought. She quickly got her helmet on and listened to the instructions from the guide.

"There are landing ports at the end of each course where you can rest if you need to. Just make sure you unclip from the top and move out of the way so others can go ahead of you," the guide said.

The men soon joined the women and Falcone jumped to the front of the line. "We need a man first in line to lead the way," he said and thumped his chest like Tarzan.

"Oh brother," muttered Anna, "Here we go… Mr. Machismo!" Rena laughed. The other guys joined in laughing and pretending to be the first in line. "Fine," said Anna laughingly.   "You guys can go first, but don't hold us up!"

"On second thought," said Falcone, "You and Rena can go first. Better view." He smiled devilishly. Anna's face displayed a look of disgust and Rena burst out laughing.

"I'll go last," Rena said. "You can be first in line Falcone."

"Ugh yah," said Anna, "*Please*- go first," and walked to

the back of the line to stand beside Rena. The rest of the group laughed and Rena and Anna let them go ahead.

"Better this way," Rena said to Anna. "I'm still a bit afraid of heights."

"Geeze Rena," Anna said, "I forgot! I feel terrible. Are you sure you want to do this?"

"Yes, I do," I need to get over this," Rena said sounding more confident than she felt. "I'm sure it will be okay."

Anna looked at her intently. "Well let me know if you want to stop at any point, okay?" "You don't have to prove anything to anyone."

"I know," Rena said. "Don't worry about me."

They followed the men and climbed up a long ladder to begin the first trek. Rena hadn't the courage to look down. She breathed a sigh of relief when she got to the platform at the top. She had made it. The first trek had them walking across a suspended wooden bridge high in the trees. They had netting on each side and rope handle rails. Their harnesses were attached at the top to a rope at all times, and Rena maneuvered through the first section following Anna quickly. "This is okay," she thought. "I can do this." At the end of the first trek, they were on a small platform. Anna turned to look at her.

"Isn't this awesome?" she said smiling. "Look at the trees, it is amazing."

Rena looked around and had to agree. Being up within the trees was amazing. It made her feel like she was a part of them.

The sun shone down from in between branches and the leaves rustled in a refreshing breeze. Rena closed her eyes and inhaled deeply. It was peaceful. As long as she didn't have to look down, she would be okay. Rena glanced beyond Anna at the second trek. Some of the guys were just finishing the second trek and Falcone and a few others were ahead of them on other treks higher in the trees. Anna and Rena approached the second trek. It was also a bridge of sorts but this time there were suspended logs of wood that appeared to be going higher into the trees. The netting on the side was gone; however, it looked like the guys ahead of them were holding on to a rope line that was suspended above them. Rena felt her stomach lurch a little bit. She took a deep breath. "I can do this," she thought.

Anna started to go onto the bridge and Rena quickly followed. "The faster I do this, the better," she thought. Rena watched Anna take the first few steps and started to go. The logs were farther apart than she had expected and the first log started to sway when she stepped on it. She held on to the rope above her as she swayed. Anna was moving quickly ahead of her and Rena did not want to be far behind. She continued to follow Anna taking her time to gain her balance on each log. Halfway through the platform, Rena lifted her right foot to reach for the next step and missed the log. Her body swayed to the left and Rena grabbed the rope above her with both hands.

"Get your balance," the platform monitor called from behind her. "Put your right foot back with the left on the log."

Rena moved her right foot back but could not feel the log. "I can't find it," she called out to the monitor clinging to the rope above.

"Look down," said the monitor, "it's right there."

Rena looked down and put her foot on the log. Big mistake. The ground suddenly seemed to swell up beneath her and Rena felt a huge belt of nausea. "Oh no," she thought and started to panic.

"Keep moving down the line, there are people behind you," the monitor on the platform ahead of her called.

" I-I can't move," she called, but her voice sounded like a whisper.

"Hey, hey, look at me," the monitor called out to her. Rena looked ahead. "Keep moving, you have a few more steps, you can do it," he said reassuringly.

Anna stepped off the bridge onto the platform ahead of her and turned around. "Rena, you can do it," she said firmly. Rena took a deep breath and moved her foot to the next log. The ground swelled up again. Rena moved her other foot to the log and held on tightly to the rope as the bridge swayed.

"Keep coming," the monitor said, "three more steps."

"Com'on Rena, you can do it, you can do it," Anna said.

Rena moved to the next log gingerly. She could hear other people behind her and knew she had to move. "Two more steps," she thought. She moved to the next log.

"One more," cried Anna. Rena moved to the last log and leapt onto the platform.

Her heart was pounding and she felt out of breath. She could feel trickles of sweat running down her back and neck. Anna hugged her, pulled back, and looked at her. "See? You *did it*, Rena, you *did it*!" Anna said beaming. "Good girl," she said and hugged her again. Anna looked forward to the next trek. "The next one isn't bad, just another ladder." Rena looked up. The ladder moved up higher into the trees.

"I think I will rest here a bit Anna, you go ahead," she said.

"Are you sure?" Anna said looking at her searchingly. "Are you okay?"

"Yah, it was just a bit much for me, I just need to chill for a bit before I go further," said Rena. "I will catch up, you go ahead."

Anna hesitated. "Are you sure Rena?" "I can wait here with you, or we can go back down." "How do we get down?" Anna asked the platform monitor.

"You have to zip line down," he said.

Anna turned back to Rena. "Do you want to go down? I will go with you."

"No, Anna, you go ahead. I might follow, but if not I will get down. Don't worry about me, I am fine," said Rena trying to sound convincing. In fact, she was not fine. She couldn't imagine going up further, and the thought of zip lining down was even more frightening. "I'll be fine," she said, "Go and catch up to Falcone or we will never hear the end of it," she said trying to sound jovial.

"That is soooo true," said Anna. "If you are sure?" she looked questionably at Rena.

"Yes, sure, go silly," said Rena.

"Okay, see you in a bit," said Anna.

Anna started up the ladder and Rena moved to the side of the platform and leaned on the railing. "Can I wait here for a bit?" Rena asked the platform monitor.

"Sure," he said, "Just stay at the side so that others can get by."

CHAPTER 6

He was enjoying this. He hadn't felt this free in years. It was great to be up high in the trees, enjoying nature and pushing himself physically. He had caught up to Falcone and the two of them were well ahead of the rest of the group.

"Let's wait for the rest of the group to catch up," Falcone said.

"Sounds good," said Carl and leaned against the railing on the platform. Falcone joined him. They could see the rest of their group climbing below. "My brother is slowing down, old man," said Carl jokingly looking at Matt a couple of treks below them.

Falcone laughed. "This is one thing we can do better than him," he said. "We shall have to rub this in."

"Definitely," said Carl with a sense of satisfaction. Matt had been the older brother that Carl had looked up to his whole life. Matt had been 10 when Carl was born, and Carl had looked to him for guidance and advice many times. Everything in life had always seemed to come easy to Matt and he always seemed to get it right. The perfect marriage, perfect career, children; you name it, he had it. Carl admired him and loved him fiercely, but he had to admit that doing one thing better than Matt felt good.

"There's Bosco and Steve," gestured Falcone, "oh, and there is Anna." Carl looked down in the direction Falcone was gesturing. He could see Anna's bright pink shirt moving up towards them.

"Where is her friend?" he asked Falcone. "I don't see her."

Falcone squinted and looked down below. "I don't either," he said. "Maybe she went back down."

Carl couldn't help the feeling of disappointment that washed over him. It surprised him and bothered him all at the same time. He had been looking forward to seeing her again. The average time on this trek was three hours, and he had been sure he would see her at some point. The thought that he wouldn't again bothered him. Something was bugging him. He felt uneasy.

The last of the guys in the group climbed up the ladder to the platform. Anna's head popped up a few minutes later and she grinned at them. "Hi guys," she said.

"Having trouble catching up cousin?" teased Falcone as he helped her onto the platform.

"No, not at all," Anna said jokingly punching his arm. "I was waiting for a bit with Rena, but she told me to go ahead without her."

"Where is she?" asked Falcone.

"I left her on the platform after the second bridge," said Anna. "She's got a fear of heights and I think the swaying of the bridge spooked her a bit." "She was going to go back down."

Carl could feel his chest tighten. "Don't you have to zip line down?" he asked turning to the platform monitor.

"Yes, that is the only way down," he replied.

"You said she is afraid of heights, wouldn't zip lining down be tough on her?" Carl asked Anna.

"Oh dear," said Anna. "I shouldn't have left her, what if she didn't go down?" Anna replied nervously.

"I can check," said the platform monitor, "where did you leave her?"

"It was after the first log bridge," replied Anna.

The platform monitor spoke into his hand held radio. Carl couldn't understand much of it as it was all spoken quickly and seemed to be a dialect of Italian, but something just didn't feel right. The platform monitor turned to the group. "Your friend is still down there. She is refusing to go down." "Is she afraid of heights?" he asked.

"Yes, oh my god," said Anna panicking. "I shouldn't have listened to her, she said she was okay, but she looked pale, and... ." Her voice broke. Matt came over and put his arm around her.

"Don't worry Anna; we will go and get her," he said reassuringly, "she will be okay."

"Only one of you can go," said the monitor. "There is not enough room in the platform to have more than one extra person."

"I'll go." The words came out of his mouth before he even realized what he was saying. Come again? He was going?

"Are you sure?" said Falcone, "She doesn't know you."

"That might be better," chimed in Matt. "Carl's done a ton of rescue operations and people are usually more compliant with a stranger," he said.

"True," said Anna, "She didn't want me to help her." She turned to Carl, "are you sure?"

Carl wasn't sure, but heard himself saying that he was sure. He sounded more confident than he felt. He had met this woman for two minutes and she had affected his thoughts already. "God help me," he thought as he set up to zip line down.

CHAPTER 7

He called. She had been crying. He told her that she sounded like she had a cold. She told him she didn't have a cold. She was feeling emotional. He changed the subject quickly and asked her if she had picked up groceries for dinner. He didn't ask why she was crying. He didn't ask why she was feeling this way.

Rena was shivering. For the past hour, she had been sitting on the platform clinging to the railing. She had been profusely sweating at times and then completely chilled. They had tried to get her to zip line down, but every time she had tried, the waves of nausea had overcome her and she had had to lean over the railing and vomit. They finally gave up on her and had left her, until five minutes ago. They were getting someone to come and take her down they had said. Rena didn't know if it was possible. She was cold, scared, and embarrassed.

"Let's get you hooked up again," the platform monitor said.

Rena got up shakily. Her feet didn't feel steady and she swayed a bit before walking forward to get the safety harness on. The monitor had just clipped the harness on, when Rena felt her stomach lurch and she quickly moved to the railing to vomit.

She felt someone behind her. Warm hands gathered up her hair while she vomited down into the trees. "It's okay, let it all out," a man's voice said comfortingly. A strong arm braced her on her left side and she vomited some more.

"What a saint this person is," she thought. *You couldn't pay me anything to do this.* After about five minutes, when she finally felt like she had been completely emptied, she turned around.

"Take it slowly," he said, "Take your time."

"What a comforting, dreamy voice," she thought turning around to see her savior. Dark brown twinkling eyes, met blue wide eyes.

"You okay now?" Carl asked.

Rena's heart jumped and dropped at the same time. She wanted to cry with relief that someone had come to get her, but at the same time, she wanted to hide her face in embarrassment. Of all the men to be sick in front of, it had to be the sexy policeman. She couldn't believe it. Here she stood, drenched with sweat, shivering, and smelling like puke, and he was grinning at her and talking to her like it was all okay. She wanted to shrink into a hole and die. She felt the tears fill her eyelids.

"No, you don't, no feeling sorry for yourself," said Carl, guiding Rena to the middle of the platform.

"I, I, am a-af-fraid of h- heights," she stuttered between chattering teeth.

"A lot of people are," said Carl, grabbing her hands. "Rena, look at me," he said looking intently into her eyes. "I'm going to hold you for a bit to get you warm. Just for a bit so that you don't go into shock. Then I am going to take you down the zip line with me." He paused. "Rena, you are safe, and you are going to be fine."

Rena stared at him. His eyes were so brown, almost black. He sounded so calm that she almost believed him. "I am going to get you warm now," Carl said. He moved behind her on the platform and wrapped his arms around her body. "Just relax, breathe... slowly, in through the nose and out through the mouth, relax and breathe. You can do it Rena, relax and breathe," Carl whispered behind her ear. Rena felt a warmth crawl up her body. She shivered. "That's good, let go, relax, you are safe," Carl said. Rena could feel her shivering stop as she started to feel the warmth penetrate her. She closed her eyes. This was good. She felt warm and safe. Carl starting rubbing her arms, bringing her back to reality. "Okay Rena, we are going to get hooked up together and get you down," he said. Rena tensed. Carl turned her around slowly to face him. "Rena look at me," he said. "This is nothing to be embarrassed about, but you have had a bit of a shock, you are scared of heights, yes?" Rena nodded. "Okay, look at me," he said. "I am going to take you down the zip line with me." You will be attached to me at all times. I won't let go, you will be safe," he said confidently. He took Rena's face in his hands and tilted her head back to look up at him. "I am safe," he said. "Say it Rena, I am safe."

"I- I am s-safe," stuttered Rena looking into his eyes.

"Good, say it again," Carl ordered softly.

"I am s-safe," Rena said.

"Good girl," said Carl nodding to the platform monitor.

"We are going to get harnessed together now. I am going to take you down." You don't have to look. Just close your eyes and hold on to me." Rena nodded. She felt queasy and nervous but for some reason she felt he was telling the truth. He would get her down safely. The platform monitor hooked Rena behind Carl. Carl moved forward to the edge of the platform. "Okay Rena," he said, "Close your eyes and hold on to me." Rena wrapped her arms around Carl's back and closed her eyes.

"I am safe, I am safe, I am safe," she thought. Carl moved off the platform.

***

The minute he had left the platform, Carl felt her tense right away and her grip on this waist tightened. The five minutes down the zip line felt like hours. "This woman is terrified," thought Carl. What in the world would possess someone with a fear of heights to go tree trekking? He was relieved when they had finally got on the ground. For some reason the thought of her panicking bothered him. He didn't want her to feel that way. The staff at the venue were waiting for them and unharnessed them quickly when they reached the ground and medics rushed to Rena to wrap her in blankets and take her to a nearby ambulance. Carl squatted on the ground and took a few deep breaths. He had rescued many people before, most from more dangerous situations, but he had never felt their anguish, their panic. He had *felt* hers. It was unnerving.

He slowly got up and took a deep breath. He could see her sitting up in the ambulance. She was hooked up to an IV and sipping on water. An ambulance attendant approached him.

"Stai bene? You okay?" he asked.

"Si," said Carl and graciously took a bottle of water that was offered. He took a long sip. The cold water felt good. "Can I go check on her?" he asked, gesturing to the ambulance where Rena was.

"Si," said the attendant and started walking toward the ambulance with Carl.

As Carl approached the ambulance, relief flowed through him. She was sitting up and had some colour back in her face. She was hooked up to an IV and had a warming blanket on. The attendants were taking her vitals and asking her questions and she was responding clearly. She looked up at him when he approached. "Hi," she said a little sheepishly.

"Hi there, feeling better? he asked.

"Yes, thanks, for getting me down. I'm so embarrassed, I really appreciate it though."

"Nothing to be embarrassed about, we couldn't have you moving in there though," Carl joked.

"Yes," she smiled, "I didn't think I would ever get down." She paused. "But seriously, I am so sorry that you had to be there when I got sick, I'm sure you didn't need to see that," she said uncomfortably.

Carl laughed. "To be honest, I had a bit of a rough night last night, so, I got sick a lot this morning, and this afternoon, so I am pleased and also ashamed to say it didn't really phase me."

"Oh," Rena, said. "Okay, I guess I don't feel too bad then," she said smiling.

"God, that smile does things to me," thought Carl.

Rena looked up at him searchingly. "You can go back up there y'know," said Rena gesturing to the trees. "Anna and I really need you to beat Falcone, if he finishes first we will never hear the end of it."

Carl smiled, eyes twinkling, "Yes, that is true, that would be torture. I would rather watch someone puke than have to listen to Falcone brag about beating everyone," he said winking at her and smiling.

"Ha-ha," said Rena.

Carl paused and looked searchingly at Rena. "Look, if you're okay, I will go, but if you need me to stay here, it's fine. I don't mind at all," said Carl.

"No, seriously, you can go," said Rena, "I'm fine now."

"Are you sure?" asked Carl looking at her. He wasn't sure she was being completely truthful. "I don't want to leave you if you really need someone here. Plus, if I leave and something happens, I will get a lot of flak from Anna, and frankly she scares me a little bit," he admitted.

Rena laughed. "I'm good," she said, "I mean it. Honestly. And thanks again, I really appreciate it."

"Any time beautiful," said Carl. "You take good care of yourself."

Carl left Rena with the attendants and starting walking back toward the course. He had walked about ten feet when it hit him. "Oh my god," thought Carl to himself, "Did I just call her beautiful?"

CHAPTER 8

She knocked on the bathroom door to get in. He was swishing mouthwash in his mouth. She asked him how he slept. She asked him every morning. He gave his usual answer, "fine." Sometimes it was "fine" or "not great," or sometimes even "better." She asked why. He never knew why. Then he left the bathroom. He did not look at her even once. He did not ask her how she slept.

Rena woke up the next morning, relaxed, refreshed. "Boy do I love this bed," she thought. The bed felt comfortable, warm, like warm muscular arms enfolding her. It felt familiar, but she couldn't pinpoint why. The excitement of the other day was almost forgotten. Carl had got the staff at Albero Avventura to radio up to Anna. Once Anna had heard that Rena was being attended to by paramedics, she had come down from the trees right away, and once the medics had given the go ahead, had promptly taken Rena home. Rena had stumbled into bed when she got there, exhausted and spent, but now she felt great. She wasn't even sure why, but she did.

Rena got up, dressed, showered, and went down to the kitchen. She was starving after all the adventures the other day. Anna wasn't up yet, so Rena made a cup of tea and helped herself to some thick Italian bread with butter and marmalade. Anna jaunted into the kitchen a few minutes later, dressed in yoga pants and a t-shirt.

"Good morning bella," she said and kissed Rena on the cheek. You look so much better how are you feeling?"

"Good morning to you too, and I am feeling great!" said Rena enthusiastically.

"Thank God," said Anna, "I was so worried about you yesterday."

"Yes, sorry, I feel terrible about that Anna, you must be regretting having me here," said Rena sorely.

"Are you kidding Rena?" "That was the most excitement I have had here in ages!" "You are the talk of the town too, news spreads fast here."

"Oh great," said Rena, "that must be so embarrassing for you."

"It is awesome!" said Anna delightedly, "nobody talks about me anymore."

"Oh well," said Rena with resignation, "I guess I can live with being the talk of the town if it takes the heat off you, but seriously, why would they talk about you?"

"I don't make babies, I only *practice*," said Anna mischievously.

Rena looked at Anna doubtfully, "Anna, you don't tell people *that* do you?"

"Every chance I get," Anna replied with a wicked grin.

***

41

After breakfast and an hour of laughing and chatting, Anna mentioned that she had to some banking, so, her and Rena jumped into the Fiat and drove into town. The town of Ariano Irpino had beautiful quaint shops lining the street and parks with lush greenery and flowers, so Rena wandered around the town while Anna got her finances in order. Anna's husband Simon sent her money while he was away teaching culinary classes in Dubai, so Anna made the trip into town frequently. Rena sat on a park bench while she waited for Anna. The warm breeze moved wisps of her hair onto her face and Rena held her hair back to keep it from moving. *What was so familiar about this?* As the realization of yesterday hit her, Rena shivered. He had held her hair back when she was sick. She remembered his arms, holding her, and holding her hair back. She remembered his smile. Rena felt tears sting her eyes. *Why was he so nice to her?* He had been so kind, he had looked so worried about her, and he didn't even know her. Rena wiped away a tear from her cheek just as Anna approached.

"Hey girl, I am done, let's go shopping!" Anna said and pulled Rena up from the bench.

Rena smiled and put away all memories of the other day as they walked arm in arm to the shops.

Three hours later, Rena and Anna returned to Anna's home loaded with parcels, chicken, cheeses, and wine. They quickly put the parcels and food away and made a quick meal of salad, fried potatoes, chicken and watermelon and peaches for dessert. Half an hour later, they were walking in the village collecting money for the fiesta in the evening.

"Why are we collecting money?" Rena asked Anna as they started going house to house to collect.

"Everyone chips in here so we can have a big party," Anna said. "It's fun and brings the whole town together," she said smiling and greeting people she knew on the street.

'What a different life," thought Rena. "Anna really has the best of both worlds," she thought. She had the crazy hustle and bustle of world-renowned locations where her husband would teach and cook, and the quaint, little village where they could recuperate and wind down. After collecting the money from several families, and being invited into several homes for coffee and biscotti, Rena and Anna returned home to get ready for the fiesta. Rena quickly changed into a sporty skort and t-shirt with matching sneakers. She put her hair up in a ponytail and added a matching cap she had purchased in town. "This will be fun," she thought skipping down the stairs to meet Anna.

***

As they walked to the park for the fiesta, Anna craned her neck and starting looking around. The park was packed with people, and Rena was surprised that so many people actually lived in the village. "Who are you looking for?" asked Rena.

"Oh, sorry," said Anna, "I forgot to tell you, Falcone said he might come by with a couple of his group tonight," she said still looking around.

Rena's heart fluttered. She silently hoped and feared Carl was one of the 'group'. She wondered how she would feel when she saw him again. She was still a bit embarrassed, but part of her wanted to see him again. The girls continued to walk in the park and passed by a wheel of fortune that was crowded with spectators and participants, and lawn games where children were laughing excitedly.

Everybody was talking loudly and excitedly and the park was so crowded that Rena wondered how they could find anyone here. Her eyes darted around at all the villagers laughing, talking – and then she did a double take. There he was. She couldn't miss him. Dressed in a navy blue t-shirt that strained across his chest and khakis that silhouetted the shape of his muscular thighs he looked every bit the knight in shining armour that Rena was remembering him to be. Even though she was a bit embarrassed about the other day, she couldn't help but stare at him. Gosh, he was gorgeous. He turned to look at her. His brown eyes burned right through her, and she felt a heat penetrate her body. "Wow," she thought. *Why does he have such an effect on me?* Carl noticed her looking in his direction and smiled. Rena melted. She tugged Anna's arm without taking her eyes off Carl. "Anna, they are over there." Anna looked at Carl and saw Falcone.

"Great, let's go over there," Anna said looking at her friend. "Rena, are you okay, you are staring."

Rena shook her head. Why did he have such an effect on her? She turned to look at Anna. "I am fine, just embarrassed a bit from yesterday."

"Don't be silly," said Anna reassuringly. "Carl seems like a good guy, I don't think he even remembers it."

Rena and Anna walked up to the guys and greeted them. Falcone glanced at Rena, "Are you okay sweetie?"

"Yes, I am fine, Falcone, but thanks for asking," Rena said smiling as Falcone hugged her a bit too close.

Matt greeted Rena as she was pushing Falcone gently away. "I'm glad Carl could help out yesterday. Glad you are okay," he said gently.

"Thanks Matt," said Rena appreciating his kind words.

"I don't know what I would have done without Carl, he was wonderful," Rena said glancing at Carl.

"You did all the work," said Carl.

"I'm not so sure about that," said Rena.

Then you don't give yourself enough credit," Carl said looking into her eyes. "You're stronger than you think you are," he said. "It takes a lot of guts to face your fears. You did really well, you should be proud of yourself," he said sincerely.

The group started walking towards the Wheel of Wishes game and Rena and Carl tagged along at the back. Anna and some of the guys took turns spinning the wheel to see what prizes they could win. Rena turned to Carl, "Do you do this all the time?" she asked, "rescuing people?"

"A lot of the time," said Carl. "It's amazing what situations people find themselves in, or what situations they get into without thinking."

"It must be pretty interesting," said Rena.

"It can be," said Carl looking at her intently.

It can be. "Those words felt like they had a double meaning," thought Rena. Her body reacted by shivering.

"What do you do Rena?" asked Carl.

"Right now, nothing," said Rena sighing. "I was working, but since my husband died I've been taking a break."

"Oh," said Carl. "I'm sorry, I didn't know."

"It's fine," said Rena. "It has been awhile now, and I really should get back to work, just not sure what I really want to do anymore," she said honestly. "You know how sometimes you think you really want something, and then something in your life happens to change all that?" she asked.

"Yes, I believe I do," said Carl. He was about to say something else, when Anna ran up to Rena and grabbed her arm.

"Come on, let's go play bocce!" she cried excitedly and pulled Rena to the field.

***

He had watched her play bocce with Anna for about an hour. He couldn't take his eyes off her. He was surprised that she was a widow. He hadn't expected that. She seemed a bit young for that and he wondered what had happened. "She must have been devastated," he thought. He hadn't been sure about her. Anna seemed like a wild child and from what Carl had heard from Falcone she was spoiled and a bit entitled. He had expected Rena to be like that too. But both girls had surprised him. Sure, Anna did seem to like the finer things in life, but she seemed genuine and caring, and there was really nothing wrong with wanting all that money could give. And Rena, she was beautiful but didn't seem to know it. He wondered how long she and her husband had known each other. "Must be so hard for her to move on," he thought. Maybe they were high school sweethearts. He could see that. Rena was sweet, and hot, and who wouldn't fall for that. He would have been smitten if she had been in his high school.

After exhausting all of the games at the fiesta, the group of them went to Anna's house for bread, ricotta cheese and wine. They sat out in Anna's garden and chatted amicably. Carl stole a few glances at Rena. She seemed relaxed and happy. Her smile lit up her face and her laugh reminded him of a small child. She tugged at his heart. He felt guilty for thinking the thoughts he had of her. He was glad she was a widow. This made her safe. He couldn't try anything with her, couldn't fall for her. He knew he could never compete with a memory. It would be easier now to keep her at arm's length. "I should be happy about this," he thought, but he was not.

CHAPTER 9

Rena woke up early. She had set the alarm for 8:30. Anna had told her that the church had mass at 10:30 and Rena wanted to go. Anna had looked at her sympathetically when she had asked about it, and Rena felt a bit guilty. She knew Anna was thinking that she was missing Jarod. But Rena wanted to go to have some time to herself. Her weeks in Italy had already seemed like a whirlwind and some quiet was what she needed. Talking to Carl last night about what she was doing made her realize that she had to think about it. She couldn't hide here in Italy forever. At some point she would have to start earning a living again.

Rena took a quick shower, got dressed, gobbled down some tea and toast, and headed to the church. Anna was still sleeping and Rena was happy. Anna had apologized profusely last night for not wanting to go, but Rena hadn't minded. This would give her the thinking time she craved. Rena left Anna's house and started walking up the hill to the church. Anna had told her it would be a good twenty-minute walk, and Rena had left early, so she took her time. The walk up the hill was gorgeous and Rena admired the views and architecture of the town buildings as she went along. At the top of the hill, she stood outside the church to admire it. It was built with grey stone and had three rose windows out front on top of three bronze portals. There were three statues in the face of the church over each portal, and it was surrounded by an old stone staircase, that looked like it had been recently restored.

Rena followed some of the parishioners into the church. When she got in the church, Rena took a seat near the middle and settled in. She looked around. The church was bright with white stone walls, beautiful artistic images in the ceiling and gold statues throughout. Rena thought it was beautiful and heavenly. She knew the mass would be in Italian but that suited her perfectly. She didn't need to listen; she just wanted to be here. A few minutes later, members of the church starting coming in chatting and greeting each other with kisses. A small choir assembled themselves in the front pew, and a young man started playing the organ. The mass began and Rena listened to the beautiful voices of the readers. She couldn't understand a word but the melodic tilt of their voices drew her in.

The mass ended after 50 minutes, and Rena took her time leaving her seat. Most of the people had already left the church, but Rena wasn't ready to go yet. She stayed and watched the priest roll out a red runner in the middle of the church. It looked like velvet and Rena wondered if royalty was visiting. Soon several men came into the church with enormous bouquets of pink, white, red, and yellow flowers and several plants. Eight large arrangements were added to stands in the aisle with green plants, and on each side of the altar, huge bouquets of colourful flowers were added. Rena saw some women come into the church and start to add small vases of flowers in each of the windows. Rena breathed in the scented smell. It was wonderful. She got up slowly to go, and as she did she passed by one of the women adding another vase in the window. "Excusi," said Rena. "What is going on?" she asked gesturing to the red carpet and flowers.

"Matrimonio," said the woman with a toothy grin.

"Ah gracie," said Rena thanking the woman. A wedding.

***

He didn't wash the dishes she had used; he wouldn't touch her side of the bathroom. She would always wash his clothes, wipe his sink, clean his side of the bed, and vacuum the house. He would not do that for her. It was her mess, he had said. He told her he loved her more than she did him. How could she believe that?

Rena and Jarod's wedding had been a whirlwind. She had wanted a small intimate wedding, but Jarod had wanted to go all out, and Rena, because she had loved him so much, relented. The months up to the wedding had been crazy with more preparations than Rena had ever expected. On the day of the wedding, Rena was exhausted. The wedding was not much of a memory for Rena. There had been so many people, and so many expectations for pictures, Rena could not remember speaking to her friends. They all said her wedding had been a great time, but to Rena, it was not even a memory. They had left right after the wedding for their honeymoon taking an early bird flight to St. Martin. Rena had to admit the honeymoon had been great. Jarod had booked them into a five-star resort and Rena had been delighted at the room, the beach, and the sun. She and Jarod had enjoyed themselves, eating and sunbathing and had met several other couples also on honeymoon. If Rena could have looked back then, she would have realized that they had spent more time hanging out with other couples than with each other. But she had been blinded by love and didn't notice a thing. That changed after the honeymoon. It was the after that she remembered the most. It was the after that hurt the most.

CHAPTER 10

As she walked down the hill from the church, Rena pushed all thoughts of her wedding aside. She didn't want to think about it anymore. She looked around enjoying the scenery as she walked. The town was built on a mountain and the views gave her a sense of peace and tranquility. She stared at the scenery while she walked. "Umph," Rena exclaimed as she was knocked to the ground. She wasn't sure what had happened. A bicycle was lying beside her wheels spinning and a teenage boy was getting himself up.

"Scusa signora non ti ho visto," the boy said.

"Sorry," Rena said trying to get up, "I didn't see you, are you okay?"

"Yes, it is my fault," he said in perfect English, "I wasn't paying attention." "Are you hurt?" the boy asked.

"No, ow," Rena said as she put too much weight on her wrist to get up. "I am okay," she said. Rena tried to get up again and was helped by strong arms that slipped under her arms from behind her. They felt familiar somehow.

"What's going on here?" said a familiar voice. Rena turned to look at Carl. He was glaring at the boy.

"It's okay," said Rena, "I wasn't looking," she said.

"No, it isn't," said Carl in a stern voice. "I saw what happened. He plowed right into you," he said his eyes glowering at the boy.

"I'm sorry," said the boy. "I didn't mean to hurt her, I wasn't paying attention," he said in a small voice.

Carl turned to Rena, "Are you okay, you're not hurt?" he asked looking into her eyes searchingly.

Rena wanted to melt. His eyes bore into her like hot coals. "I think he likes me," she thought for a fleeting second. A quick shake from Carl on either side of her arms brought her quickly back into reality.

"Rena?" he asked.

"Yes, yes I am fine… I wasn't looking either… daydreaming," she said with a small smile.

"Okay," Carl said. "You can go," he said to the boy, "but pay attention, next time you could really hurt someone or even get yourself hurt."

"Yes," said the boy and quickly got on his bike and tore away.

Rena looked at Carl. He looked back at her. "You seem to always be rescuing me," she said with a shy smile.

"Do you need *rescuing* Rena?" Carl said still looking into her eyes.

Rena felt the heat quickly rise in her body. The way he had said that, *rescuing* did all sorts of things to her. "Ah,"

Rena stumbled on her words. He was looking at her so intently that she felt he could read her mind. He smiled.

"Coffee?" he asked.

"Coffee," repeated Rena. She couldn't stop looking at his mouth. He had such a great mouth. Full lips, white teeth, and the dimples that surrounded that smile, they were nice dimples. *I wonder what he can do with that mouth*, thought Rena. The thought immediately brought warmth all over her body and she felt moistness between her legs. "What is this guy doing to me?" she thought.

"Rena?" Carl moved his had to touch the side of her face. "Are you okay? Coffee?" he asked.

"Ah yes," said Rena, the moment broken. "Yes, coffee sounds good, let's go," she said.

Carl smiled. "Great, he said, let's go."

I think he can read my mind, she thought.

***

They ducked into a small café near the bottom of the hill. It was already starting to get warm outside so they went inside and took a small table near the window. They sipped espresso, ate lemon biscotti, and chatted amicably about what they thought of Italy so far, places they both knew in Toronto, and the work that Carl and the other police officers were doing in Bicarri. Rena felt comfortable. It was easy to talk to Carl. He listened intently and asked so many questions. He let her ask him questions. It was fun. The café started to get busy. People started bustling in and taking the tables on the patio. A procession of villagers all dressed in their finest starting walking up the hill.

"Must be for the wedding," Carl remarked looking out the window. "Want to go watch?" he asked.

"You knew about the wedding?" Rena asked surprised.

Carl nodded, "Yes, Falcone mentioned that it would be neat to watch." "It's a big village celebration here, not like my wedding," he said.

Rena's heart dropped. He was married? Funny how that thought had never occurred to her. Then again, of course he was. He was kind, thoughtful, and incredibly hunky. "Nobody would let that get away," she thought.

"Does your wife mind you being away so long?" Rena asked.

"What?" Carl said turning back to look at her. "No, I'm not married anymore. Divorced. Nine years ago."

"Oh, sorry," said Rena.

"Things happen for a reason Rena," Carl said pinching her cheek as he got up. He put money on the table and reached for her hand. "C'mon, let's go watch."

They stood on the street with other spectators and watched the wedding procession go up the hill. The bride came in an old-fashioned open car. She looked gorgeous and waved and smiled as all of the spectators cheered her on.

"Yup, definitely not my wedding," grinned Carl.

Rena laughed, "Not mine either." "Maybe mine would have been better with a whole town to support me," blurted Rena.

Carl stopped. He looked at Rena smiling at the wedding

procession. Had he heard that correctly? He wasn't sure she had meant to say that out loud, or maybe she hadn't realized she had. *This could change everything,* he thought.

He had been pleased to see her on the hill this morning. He had stood and admired her walking down the hill. She had a great curvaceous body and he had felt a bit guilty of the thoughts that had run through his head. It seemed wrong to think of these things with her husband watching down on her from the heavens. When he had seen the bike racing in her direction he had wanted to call out to her. But nothing came out. He felt helpless as he saw her get hit and fall. He had rushed to her side his heart pounding at every step. When he had seen her lying on the ground all crumpled, he had felt sick. But when she started to get up, the pounding in his chest had slowed down, and he realized she was okay. He felt an immense pull to her. When she looked at him with her deep blue eyes, he wanted to hold her in his arms and make it all better. But he knew she was a widow, probably getting over the love of her life, and that is what stopped him. But what she had just said could change everything. What if everything hadn't been all rosy? The realization that this could be true made him feel elated. What was it about this woman that drew him to her? He wanted to figure it out, find out everything about her. At the same time, he was terrified. He had fallen like this before and it had ended badly. Why would this time be any different?

The wedding procession had moved up the hill, and Rena turned to look at Carl. "That was great!" she exclaimed with a big smile.

"God she is beautiful when she smiles," thought Carl.

"I should get back to Anna though, she will be worried about me," Rena said.

"Let me walk you back," said Carl, "God knows what kind of trouble you will get into on the way home," he said grinning.

Rena laughed. Her laugh sounded childlike. Carl loved it. They continued down the hill and onto the street where Anna lived. "How long are you here for Rena?" Carl asked.

"I'm not sure," Rena said. "I didn't book a return flight. Anna told me I could stay as long as I needed to. "When are you going back to Bicarri?" Rena asked.

"Not for a week or so," said Carl. "My brother and some of the other guys are leaving here tonight. Falcone is taking them to the airport. He has to get his parents from the airport so it makes sense," said Carl.

"You didn't want to go?" asked Rena.

"Not enough room in his car," Carl said while laughing. "That is partly true," he thought. The guys were all a bit bulky and did have a lot of luggage, but Falcone was taking a SUV. Carl could have squeezed in, but the thought of maybe bumping into Rena again, made him decide not to go. It gave him two days to be on his own. Two days to figure out why he was so attracted to Rena. Two days to figure out what he was going to do about it.

They arrived at Anna's doorstep and Rena grabbed the door to go in.

"Rena, wait," Carl said.

"Aren't you coming in?" said Rena. "I'm going to go for a run," he said. "All this great Italian food needs to be run off," he said patting his stomach.

"You look pretty fit to me," Rena said.

Carl felt his tummy tighten. *Was she coming on to him?* "Thanks," he said leaning forward kissing Rena on the cheek. "See you later beautiful," he said.

"See you later," she said smiling and went into the house.

CHAPTER 11

Rena closed the front door to Anna's house and leaned against it. *Oh my God*, she thought. He had kissed her! Sure, it had been a peck on the cheek, but he had called her beautiful and he had kissed her. She shouldn't feel so elated. It could mean nothing, but it made her feel good. She liked it. She liked him.

Rena walked into the house calling for Anna. "In here," Anna said calling from the kitchen. She was busy baking. There were bowls and pans everywhere and Rena could see remnants of flour in her hair. Rena laughed.

"Anna, what are you doing?" she said.

"Baking, baking and more baking," said Anna. "This is what happens when I don't go away with Simon." "I bake and bake and get fat, and bake some more!" Anna wailed.

Rena walked up to Anna and gave her a big hug. "Oh Anna, you should go and see Simon."

"But I have you here Rena," Anna said. "I can't just up and go, and I don't want you to leave, you need this."

"Can't I stay here while you go?" Rena asked. She didn't want to leave either. She wasn't ready to go back to Toronto yet.

"Of course you can," said Anna, "But I can't leave you alone."

"Sure you can," said Rena. "I'll be fine."

"But nobody is here," said Anna. "Falcone is off to Rome for a few days to get his parents." "There would be nobody here if you needed anything," she said.

"What about Uncle, I mean, Zio Augusto?" Rena said. She hadn't seen Anna's uncle since the first day he had dropped her off to Anna's place.

Anna laughed. "That's Falcone's dad Rena!" she exclaimed.

"What?" said Rena. "I didn't know that," she said.

Anna grinned. "He left with my Zia for New York the day after you came," she said. "He was smitten with you. I think he has high hopes for you and Falcone."

Rena laughed. She could see where Falcone got his style from. Zio Augusto had called Rena "Bella" the whole ride from Rome to Ariana Irpino and had kissed her cheeks several times when they had arrived at Anna's that evening.

"So see?" said Anna, "Nobody is here."

"Carl's here," blurted Rena. She hadn't meant to tell Anna and she wasn't sure why, but now seemed like a good time. "He's staying at Falcone's parents place."

"How do you know that?" said Anna inquisitively.

Rena giggled. "He saved me from another episode

again."

"What? Rena what happened?" said Anna, pushing Rena onto a chair and sitting to face her.

Rena told Anna the whole story, and mentioned the coffee afterwards as well. She left the kiss out. She wasn't sure she wanted to share that.

"Geeze Rena, promise me you will start being more careful."

"I will," said Rena. "But see? I won't be here alone." I can always call Carl if I need him."

"I guess so," said Anna somewhat reluctantly. "Let me invite him over for lunch." "I want to make sure he has good intentions for you," she said determinedly.

***

Carl came over for lunch and Anna gave him the third degree. Rena almost felt like she wasn't there with the two of them talking about her. "I don't want Rena sitting here alone, she needs to get out and enjoy and see things. You will take her out, right?" said Anna.

"Anna!" exclaimed Rena. She was embarrassed. Anna was making her sound helpless and feeble, and more like a little child than a grown woman. "I can take care of myself and entertain myself y'know," she said. She saw Carl turn away with a smirk. *He thinks this is funny*, she thought. Anna came over to where Rena was sitting and hugged her.

"I know you can take care of yourself Rena," she said and hugged her again. "I'm sorry, I am feeling bad since I am going away," she said.

"Maybe you need a puppy," teased Carl.

Rena and Anna laughed. Rena hugged Anna back and gave her a kiss on the cheek. "You're a super friend and thanks for thinking of me. I am grateful to be here. Now go and see your husband and don't worry about me!" she ordered with a smile.

"Okay, okay," said Anna, "I won't worry." She turned around to get a cake out of the oven.

"I will take good care of her," said Carl and winked at Rena.

Rena could have sworn that what he had said held some innuendo. She felt the heat rise in her body.

"Let me help you Anna," she said and getting up from the table.

An hour later, promising to call the next day, Carl had left and Rena was sitting with Anna in her room helping her pack. Before he left, Carl had kissed both girls on the cheeks. He lingered a little longer on Rena's cheeks and she had felt her face turn red as Anna gave her an odd look. Sitting on Anna's bed now, she was relaxed and enjoying the time with her friend. Anna was trying to pick out elegant dresses for a couple of balls her and Simon would attend.

"Is this one okay?" she asked holding up a shimmering long peach coloured dress against her.

"Is it okay?" "It is gorgeous!" Rena said gasping. She had never seen a dress so beautiful. "Is it made of diamonds?"

Anna laughed. "Yah, it's is definitely gorgeous," she said rolling her r's. "It's couture. I got it the last time Simon and I were in Paris." "Speaking about gorgeous," she said sitting on the bed with Rena, "I couldn't help but notice that you turned a little red when Carl kissed you. Do you have a crush on him?"

"What? No, well, not really. I don't know," said Rena brushing it off.

"I don't know his story," said Anna. "Falcone really never mentioned him, or maybe he did once or twice but I can't remember. Just be careful, some of these guys are just out for a good time," she warned. "Although... that might be just what you need," she said with a mischievous grin.

"Ha-ha, probably," laughed Rena.

Anna got up and pulled out another dress and soon the topic of Carl was forgotten. Rena was happy that Anna got distracted. She didn't quite know what she thought of Carl or why she reacted the way she did to him. "He might just be out for a good time," she thought. And really, what was so bad about that? It had been awhile, it might be nice to get laid. Then again, Rena had never been good at one-night stands. Not that she really had ever had any. She hadn't been with a lot of men, but with the ones she had; most of them had been study group friends from university. After a night of studying, they would end up drinking and a few times, she ended up in bed with one of them. Rena always found it hard to separate the friendship from the sex afterwards. It felt awkward. But that was before Jarod. After him, there had been no one.

CHAPTER 12

Anna left in her Fiat bright and early the next morning to catch a flight to Dubai. The little car was stuffed to the brim with two suitcases and a few bags. Anna was not one for packing light. Rena stood at the door of Anna's house and waved until she couldn't see the Fiat anymore. She turned and walked into the house and closed the door. The house already felt quiet without Anna and her bustling personality. But it wasn't a bad quiet. Rena hadn't really had much time to herself since she came to Italy. It would be nice to relax in a warm bath with a good book.

Rena went up the stairs to her bedroom and grabbed her book and her robe. She grabbed her cell phone in case Carl called, although it would probably be a couple of hours before he did, she thought. She approached the deep round marble tub and turned on the water. Anna had several bottles on the ledge of the tub and Rena opened each one to smell them. Ah, lavender, she inhaled the scent deeply and poured some of the salts into the bath. She got undressed and got herself into the tub. It felt great.

***

He called her on his way home from work. He always did, like clockwork. He always said the same thing, "Hi Rena bena." She always asked him about his day. He never said much. He would ask her but she knew he wasn't listening. This was the only time he spoke to her. He didn't have to look at her over the phone.

"Rena."

Rena could hear him. "Sheesh, Jarod," she thought. What do you want? "I must have done something wrong again," she thought. She opened her mouth to call him, but nothing came out. "Jarod?" Rena woke up with a start and knocked her book and phone into the tub. "Oh crap," she said as she tried to fish them out. The tub was deep and full of bubbles and Rena couldn't find either item quickly. She paused. She heard someone running up the stairs.

"Rena, Rena, are you okay?"

Oh my god, the realization hit her. Carl was coming up! "I'm, ah," Rena stood up and then promptly slid back into the tub.

Carl opened the door to the bathroom and Rena sank down into the bubbles. "Oh, geeze, sorry," Carl turned his head away from Rena and looked at the door. "I heard you call out, are you okay?" he asked.

"Umm, yes," said Rena sitting up and fishing around for her phone. Carl started to turn and Rena sank back down under the bubbles.

"Are you sure?" he said. "I've been calling you for the past couple of hours and you didn't pick up. I got worried, and well, frightened of the wrath of Anna if anything happened to you," he said and grinned.

65

"I didn't hear it," Rena said somewhat accusingly. Two hours?

"Let me see it," said Carl gesturing for her to hand him the phone.

"I'm trying to find it," Rena said. Carl look puzzled.

"It's in the tub," Rena said disgustedly as she found her soaked book and let it land on the floor outside the tub with a thud. Carl burst out laughing. "It's not funny, you startled me," said Rena trying not to laugh herself.

"I can help you find it," Carl said approaching the tub.

"No!" said Rena. "Get out, I will find it."

"Okay, okay, just trying to make amends," said Carl grinning. He walked towards the bathroom door and turned around, "Oh yah, get dressed, we are going to Pompeii."

***

The drive to Pompeii was beautiful. The scenery was outstanding and Carl wasn't just thinking about the view. Rena sat beside him in Falcone's Fiat. She looked out at the mountains and flowers remarking here and there, about what she saw. Carl shook his head and concentrated on the road. The mental picture of her in the tub kept flashing through his mind. He had been worried when he hadn't got hold of her. She seemed a bit accident prone and all kinds of things had gone through his head before he couldn't stand it anymore and knew he had to go to Anna's to see if she was okay. When he heard her cry out, he ran up the stairs, worried, that she had hurt herself again. But there she was, covered in bubbles, well, not fully covered, and looking like a beautiful angry nymph. It was breathtaking. He had wanted to take her out of the tub and to bed then and there. He felt his shorts tighten near his crotch. He couldn't think of this while he was driving. She had some kind of spell on him, and he wasn't scared. He wanted to know everything about her. He may have lost his mind, but if it was the last thing he did in Italy, he was going to know it all.

They arrived in Pompeii two hours later. It was sweltering. The sun was beating down like a furnace and Carl felt like he was going to melt. They walked in and around the amphitheater marveling at the craftsmanship. They viewed many old buildings and ruins and chatted about what life might have been there. They finally ducked into an air-conditioned museum and both Carl and Rena sighed with delight to feel the coolness on their skin. They followed a tour group and watched a video presentation about the area and its history. The museum had statues, paintings and drawings on loan from Berlin, Germany and Carl was enthralled taking Rena through the many halls of the museum. He loved things of beauty, and art and history fascinated him. He could feel Rena looking at him intently. "I guess I didn't strike you as an art and history buff eh?" he asked looking at her.

"No, not at all," said Rena smiling, "But it is a nice surprise. Maybe you can teach me a few things," she said gesturing at the paintings around them.

"Maybe I can," Carl murmured. He could tell the air conditioning was on full blast in the museum but he still felt hot. Every time he thought of Rena or looked at her, he felt the heat. This was going to be a long day.

After exiting the museum, the two of them decided to go for a drink. They stopped at an outdoor café and ordered tall glasses of beer and water with lemon. Rena took a long sip of her beer. "Ahhh," she said. "Nectar of the gods," she said giggling. Carl looked at her stupefied. "Carl, are you okay?" she asked noting his frozen look.

How can she ask that? thought Carl. Watching her chug that beer and seeing her swallow the cool beverage was driving him crazy. He had officially lost it. He knew it. He smiled at her. "I'm great," he said smiling at her.

"Me too," she said grinning back at him.

They finished their drinks and kept the conversation light. Although it was still hot and not too comfortable outside, Carl didn't want this day to end. "Do you want to get close up to Mount Vesuvius?" he asked Rena. It would probably be cooler near there and would give him more time with her.

"I would love to," said Rena excitedly. "I have always wanted to go. This is so great!"

Carl loved her enthusiasm. Everything seemed like such a treat to her. And she couldn't stop thanking him. She had thanked him when they drove in to Pompeii, thanked him when they saw the amphitheater, thanked him at the museum, thanked him for the beer. He was beginning to think that she had never been taken anywhere. But that was impossible. No man would want to share her, but he definitely would want to show her off. Her husband must have taken her out to see shows, theatre, dinner, vacations. He must have.

***

The drive to Mount Vesuvius was quick and soon they were at the bottom of the mountainous volcano. They parked the car and got out to look at the volcano. Rena looked in awe at its majestic form. "I didn't realize it was so big," she said, "and that it would actually look like a volcano." She wasn't sure what she had pictured, but here it was, and it was beautiful.

"It's pretty amazing," said Carl looking up at it.

Rena noticed cars travelling up the mountain. "Oh, you can drive up there," she said pointing to Carl.

Carl had noticed before and had actually heard about this. But he wasn't risking Rena having an attack so he had decided not to mention it. "Yes," he said briefly and brushed the thought aside.

"Do you want to drive up?" Rena asked.

"No, this is good," Carl said turning to look at her and brushing her cheek with his hand

We can go," she said looking at him.

"Look Rena," Carl said looking serious. "You don't have to pretend to be something you're not with me. It's okay to be scared. I'm enjoying today, being with you. I don't need to go up a mountain."

"Okay," said Rena, "I understand, and this might sound crazy but, I actually *want* to go up there."

Carl gave her such a look that if Rena wasn't trying to convey her seriousness to him she might have laughed. "Rena, let's not play games, you don't have to do this," he said. He sounded a bit perturbed.

"I'm not playing games, I seriously want to go," said Rena feeling her temper rise. "For some reason I don't feel scared around you, I feel safe and I want to try it. But if you would rather not, then let's just go," she said hotly. It was a hot day and she had had enough. Jarod had never listened or believed a word she said. Nobody trusted her to make her own decisions. She had actually really wanted to go up that mountain. That had shocked and surprised her, and made her feel exited and strong. Now Carl was ruining it by throwing her fears back at her. She started to walk away and Carl grabbed her arm and turned her around to look at him.

"Rena, don't walk away. I'm sorry if I said something wrong. I'm just worried about you."

"Why does nobody trust me to make my own decisions?" asked Rena. "Anna thinks I cannot take care of myself, you think I am an accident prone freak; why won't anyone just listen to me?"

Carl looked at her and sighed. "You're right Rena. I think everyone wants to protect you. We all know you have been through a lot. It's natural for people who love you to do that," he said. "But, you make a good point. If you want to go up then let's go. But you have to promise me, if at any point you start to feel like you need to go back down, you will let me know right away. Deal?"

"Deal," said Rena nodding her head.

"Okay let's go then," Carl said opening the car door.

Rena got in the car and waited for Carl to get in on his side and start the car. He got in and turned to look at Rena. "Ready?" he said throwing her a stunning smile.

"Ready," she said smiling back.

Carl started the drive up the mountain and Rena could feel her heart pounding, but it was not from the drive. *It's natural for people who love you to do that*, he had said. *Holy crap*, thought Rena smiling.

CHAPTER 13

The winding drive up Mount Vesuvius was slow and Rena took her time to enjoy the view. At the first lookout point, Carl stopped the car and they both got out to have a look. Rena stood at the barrier fence and looked out. "Okay, this is a little high," she thought. Carl came up behind her.

"You okay?" he asked gently.

"Yes, maybe a little queasy," she admitted. Carl stood behind her and put her arms around her waist.

"How's this?" he asked.

Rena leaned back on him. "It's good," she said. She could feel his breath on her neck. The air on the mountain was cool and his breath was like fire on her neck. She could feel his lips brush the nape of her neck, and then feel him move his head beside hers. "It's so beautiful, almost breathtaking," she said.

"Yes, absolutely," said Carl whispering close to her ear. "Rena, I'm so glad I got to do this with you," he said tightening his hold on her.

"Me too," said Rena and snuggled in a bit closer to him. "I don't think I could have done this without you," she said.

***

After driving down Mount Vesuvius Carl and Rena drove to a small restaurant with a view of the mountain. It was nice to finally be in the air conditioning again. They both ordered tall glasses of water and chatted a bit about the area, as they munched on Italian bread, ricotta and tomato salad, and olives. Carl talked to their waiter in Italian, who suggested they go to Pozuolli and see the Solfatara Caldera.

"What is it?" asked Rena leaning forward on the table.

"It's a volcano. You can see vents of steam coming up from the ground. It's about 20 minutes' drive from here, what do you think?" asked Carl.

"Let's go," said Rena.

She felt rejuvenated from the refreshments and didn't want her day with Carl to end too soon. Carl paid the bill, thanked the waiter and they got back into the Fiat. The drive to the Solfatara Caldera was scenic and Carl and Rena chatted amicably. They hadn't talked more about the conversation on the mountain, but Rena kept replaying it in her mind. *It's natural for people who love you to do that.*

"What are you thinking about?" asked Carl as the Fiat stopped at a turn.

Rena looked at him, smiling, "Nothing," she said.

"Nothing?" Carl said and lifted his eyebrows.

Well, not quite nothing, she thought. "Just day dreaming, that's all," she said with a mischievous grin.

"I would like to get on that train," said Carl, moving quickly as a car honked behind them. "We shall *revisit* this," he said. Rena shivered. Not a cold shiver, but a *good* shiver.

They arrived at Solfatara Caldera and on getting out of the Fiat; the smell of the sulfur coming from the mud pits accosted them. "If it smells this bad here, I can't imagine the smell when we get closer," said Rena, lifting the collar of her shirt to cover her nose. Carl laughed. She looked like a young child who didn't like the smell of their supper. The smell didn't bother him that much. He had been in many locker rooms, and this wasn't all that bad. They paid for tickets and waited for their tour to begin. A young man greeted them and a group of ten others to begin the tour.

As they started walking towards a hot pool of boiling sulfur in the ground, Carl began to think that the smell might just be a bit worse than what he had experienced before. It didn't help that it was sweltering out, and the steam from the boiling sulfur was heating the air around them. The tour continued and moved them to a dry area of land where they could see the gas from the volcano coming out of a hole. The stench was unbelievable and Carl moved his shirt up to his nose as well. Rena turned and looked at him and laughed beneath her shirt. Carl felt sheepish. This really was bad. As they continued walking, they noticed tiny lizards moving away from the hole. "Poor things can't take the smell, smart animals," he thought.

After the tour, Carl and Rena loaded back into the car. They were both drenched in sweat and the smell of sulfur still permeated their nostrils.

"Let's get the heck out of here," said Carl.

"Yes, drive fast!" said Rena.

***

Arriving back in Ariano Irpino, Carl turned onto the laneway into Anna's house. He got out of the car and opened Rena's door. "Look, we both have to eat, why don't we both wash up and meet later for meal?" he suggested.

"That sounds good," said Rena. "I feel like a big sweaty mess so I really need to shower first. Plus, I can still smell the Sulphur." Carl was amused and it must have displayed on his face as she reacted, "Seriously, I can!"

Carl laughed and put his arm around her waist and pulled her close to him. "I had a great time today Rena," he whispered into her ear.

"I'm so sweaty," said Rena moving a little bit in his grasp.

Carl moved his other arm around her waist and pulled her closer. "Me too," he said and moved his lips toward hers.

His lips touched hers gently, almost teasing, barely there. "Rena, can I kiss you?" he asked.

"Yes," Rena said forgetting her sweaty clothes.

She felt his hand move up her body from her waist to the back of her head. He moved his hand to cup her hair and moved her gently forward to meet him. His tongue gently teased her lips open and moved expertly in her mouth. His lips teased and commanded at the same time. Rena responded. Their tongues collided and Rena felt a moistness penetrate between her legs. His lips moved from her mouth to her neck and back again. His tongue demanded more. Rena felt like she was on fire. She melted into this body and could feel his hardness pressing against her. She responded more urgently to his kisses and he responded by plunging his tongue deeper into her mouth. Her hands moved through his hair and she could feel his hands move up and down her back and then cup her bottom. She could hear him sigh. He held her close and kissed her neck gently.

"Rena, what are you doing to me?" he said. He grasped her head gently in his hands and turned it up to look at him. She could feel his chest breathing heavily against her breasts. "You are so sweet, you make me feel alive again," he said caressing her cheek. Rena could feel tears come to her eyes. Nobody had ever said anything like this to her before. *Nobody*. He kissed her again and gently pulled away holding her hands at arm's length. "I really need to take a shower now," he said staring into her eyes.

Rena smiled, "Yah, me too."

"I'll be back for you," he said and gave her a quick kiss.

"You better," she said smiling and walked into the house.

***

Carl turned the shower on cold and let the water pour down his body. He gasped as the water touched his groin. He wasn't sure he had ever been quite this hard and turned on before and the fact that it was 42 degrees Celsius outside didn't help. God, what Rena did to him. He hadn't planned for any of this. Well, to be honest, he hadn't planned anything. This was unusual for him. He usually had a plan of attack to court a woman and get her into bed. But he hadn't felt like that with Rena. He *wanted* to get to know her. He *had* to get to know her. It was strange, foreign, familiar, and scary all at the same time. He had vowed not to fall in love again, not to let another woman steal his heart. But Rena hadn't stolen it; somehow, in the last week since he had met her, she had *possessed* it. She held it in the palm of her hand and Carl couldn't do anything about it. He was helpless and vulnerable. And he had never felt better about it in all his life.

CHAPTER 14

Carl arrived at Anna's place and Rena peaked out the window to see what he was wearing. He hadn't said where they were going, and Rena hadn't really known what to wear. She had looked at the meager items of clothing she had brought to Italy and had decided to have a look in Anna's closet instead. She knew Anna wouldn't mind. In fact, Anna would probably encourage it! Rena tried on many items and finally decided on a pale blue A-line sleeveless dress. It was hot enough and she wanted to be as cool as possible. The skirt flowed around her and the dress fit her well. Rena looked in the mirror and was pleased with what she saw. She had searched in Anna's closet and had found silver strappy sandals and pretty white ballerina flats. She couldn't decide so she thought she would wait to see what Carl was waiting before she chose. She grabbed a white backpack purse from Anna's closet, stuffed her incidentals inside, and went to wait at the front window.

He climbed out of the Fiat. Rena saw his muscular legs first. God, he was gorgeous. He was wearing navy blue dress shorts and a blue and white checked shirt. Rena

77

quickly put the flats on and went to the door. She opened the door before Carl got there and smiled.

"Hi beautiful," Carl said.

"Hi beautiful," said Rena smiling.

Carl leaned in and gave her a quick kiss. "You look beautiful in blue Rena," he said.

"*You* look beautiful in blue Carl," Rena echoed back.

"Let's skip dinner Rena," Carl said with a smoldering look in his eyes.

"Let's...ah," Rena stumbled and laughed.

Carl grinned mischievously. "Gotcha."

"Yes, you did," Rena said smiling.

"Hungry?" Carl asked.

"Starving."

Carl drove the Fiat for nearly an hour to the neighbouring town of Castelfranci. The restaurant was built out of old grey stone and was surrounded by beautiful grounds with streams, romantic gazebos and flowers.

"I heard about this place from Uncle Augusto," Carl said as he opened the door for Rena.

"You call him Uncle Augusto too?" Rena asked.

"No, I don't, but he told me that is what you call him, he said hello by the way," Carl said grinning. Rena laughed. The evening was starting out great and she felt comfortable. She had wondered how it would be after the steamy kiss, but things seemed natural and the conversation was flowing easily.

Carl opened the restaurant door for Rena. It was an old heavy wooden door. Scents and aromas of herbs, meats and spices assaulted Rena's nostrils. Her stomach growled. "It smells great in here," she said. The foyer was narrow barely wider than the width of the door and a maître de stood at a podium. Carl moved Rena up closer to the podium. He spoke Italian to maître de who smiled and starting happily chatting with Carl. Rena had no clue what they were talking about, and she didn't even care. She was fascinated. Beyond the maître de, she could see the kitchen. Fresh herbs were hung from the ceiling to be dried, and it was bustling with activity. Pots and pans were being moved from stove to stove and Rena could chefs busy plating and tasting.

"Com'on beautiful," Carl whispered into her ear and guided her to follow the maître de. The restaurant inside had amber stone walls and archways that defined entrances to small rooms that held a few tables. Each room had a stone fireplace. It was candlelit and romantic and Rena could hear the murmured conversations of the other patrons. The maître de brought them to a secluded corner in a back room where they had privacy but could see the full restaurant.

"This is just lovely," Rena said as she sat down in her seat.

"Yes, it is quite something. The building has been here since 1834. Thankfully it wasn't damaged in the earthquake they had here in the 90s," said Carl. "Apparently it has been in the family for generations."

"It's wonderful," said Rena looking around and smiling. At this moment, she felt truly happy.

They enjoyed a quiet meal of potato gnocchi in a red sauce, grilled lamb, zucchini flowers, asparagus and red wine. Rena felt like this was the best she had ever eaten. She wasn't sure if it was because she had such a tiring day, but the food seemed tastier than she had ever had before. She chatted amicably with Carl about her and Anna's adventures in university, and Carl chimed in with a few stories of Falcone's first few days on the force. After a dessert of espresso, Carl looked intently at Rena.

"You know I really enjoy your company Rena," said Carl, "And I want to get to know you better. But."

"But?" Rena asked, her heart stopping for a minute.

Carl sighed. "But, I don't want to push you into something you're not ready for. I know your husband died not too long ago."

He kept looking at her and Rena felt her insides die. *He pities me,* she thought. *He pities me but he doesn't know the truth. If I told him he would probably hate me,* she thought.

"What are you thinking," Carl asked interrupting Rena's thoughts.

"Ugh," Rena said, not meaning for it to come out loud. "I guess I didn't want to have this conversation," she said.

"Did I upset you?" asked Carl. "If I'm overstepping my bounds in any way Rena, please let me know," he said.

"No, it's not that." It's just, that we have been having so much fun, and now it feels serious," Rena blurted out.

"Do you just want fun, Rena?" he asked. "I can do that, but I have to admit, I want more."

"No," Rena shook her head. "I want more too," it's just

that I am not used to talking about stuff like this," she said feeling foolish.

"What do you mean," asked Carl looking puzzled. "You and your husband never talked about your feelings?"

"We did, at the beginning," said Rena, but..."

Before she could finish three waiters came out of the kitchen with a plate of tiramisu with sparklers on top. They were singing an Italian song and clapping their hands. They put the dessert on the table and the whole restaurant clapped. Rena laughed looking at Carl. "What was that about?" she asked him thanking the waiters.

Carl laughed, "I have no idea really, I couldn't understand the song, but it was great."

Rena laughed. It was great. The atmosphere had changed.

They finished their dessert and left the restaurant thanking the waiters and maître de on the way out. Rena felt stuffed. Carl suggested they take a walk around the laneway and gardens that were lit up with yellow lights. He grasped her hand and they walked and laughed about the singing, making up reasons for what it meant.

"Maybe they thought it was a birthday," said Rena.

"Not sure," said Carl, "but they didn't sing the word birthday. I don't know," he said and laughed.

They walked around the grounds and back to the car. Rena walked to her side of the Fiat and Carl followed. He turned her around against the car and kissed her, his tongue exploring her mouth sensuously. "That's enough for now," said Carl in a rough voice, "We need to be somewhere more private." He opened her door and Rena got into the car. The kiss had opened up all of her desires again and she could feel moistness between her legs under her dress. Carl got into the driver seat, leaned forward, and kissed her again quickly. "Rena, you will be the death of me," he said. Carl reversed the Fiat and drove back to the road to Anna's town. Rena couldn't keep the smile off her face.

CHAPTER 15

Carl drove onto the laneway in front of Anna's house and parked. "Coffee?" asked Rena. She didn't want this day to end.

Carl smiled. "Yes, coffee," he said.

Rena could swear he made it sound all innuendo- like but she wasn't sure. Carl got out of the car and opened the door for Rena. He helped her out and held her hand, and they walked into the house together. In the kitchen, Rena started looking for Anna's coffee maker. "I could have sworn she had one somewhere," she said opening cupboards, as Carl looked on amused.

"Are you sure she has one?" he asked sitting on kitchen chair leaning back comfortably.

Rena turned around. She could hear the amusement in his voice. "Look, I know you think she doesn't have one, and only uses those espresso thingy's, but she has been making me coffee so she must have one." Rena turned around to look in another cupboard determined to find it. All she found was espresso makers, and not just one.

Anna apparently had a thing for espresso makers as she had several of them, all in different sizes, materials and colours. Carl got up from the table and took an espresso maker from Rena's hand.

"Let me help you sweetie," he said and proceeded to put it on the stove. He expertly added water to the maker and asked Rena where the coffee was. Rena pointed it out and Carl added it to the maker. Somehow, she found this kind of sexy. She wasn't sure why. It could be the wine they had at dinner, or maybe it was the heat of the day. Either way, she was starting to feel very warm.

As if on cue, the espresso maker started to boil and Rena walked toward the stove. Carl turned the stove off and grabbed Rena and held her against the counter. He pressed against her, leaned on the counter, and started kissing her neck. "Rena, are you sure you really want coffee?" he asked.

"Umm...ah, oh god, no," I don't, oh..." Rena said as Carl moved his kisses down to her chest. "D-do you want coffee?" she asked as Carl's hand caressed her up the side of her thigh to her hip. His touch was mesmerizing her and she couldn't move. Carl's hand reached down and under her dress and moved up the side of her leg to her buttocks.

"Do you want coffee, Rena?" he asked looking into her eyes. She couldn't move. His eyes were smoldering and he looked almost dangerous. He smiled a tiny wicked smile.

He knows the effect he is having on me, she thought.

He leaned forward, pressed his lips against hers, gently at first, and then moved his tongue to slide inside her mouth. The kiss brought a heat to her body like she hadn't known before. He expertly moved his hand under her dress and cupped her buttocks, squeezing, rubbing, touching. Rena felt herself buckle in the knees. She ached to have him touch her between her legs. Carl continued to kiss her and moved his other hand to cup her left breast. She could feel her nipple harden under the silk dress. His mouth moved from her lips back to the nape of her neck. He kissed her neck, moved behind her ear, and started nibbling on it. She could feel his tongue and hot breath move around her ear causing her to release a quiet moan.

Carl stopped and looked at Rena. "Rena, I don't want coffee, I could care less about coffee, I just want you," he said in a low voice. She had never seen his eyes look so dark; they looked almost black.

"My god, he is sexy," she thought. "I, I, d-don't want c-coffee either," Rena said screaming inside silently for him to kiss her again.

Carl grabbed the back of her head and plunged his tongue into her mouth. The kiss was hot, sexy, demanding. Rena felt the heat rise between her legs. She moved her hands up and down his muscular back and down the sides of his hips. He kept kissing her and teasing her nipple. Rena felt like she was going to go mad. She moved her hands from his back to his waist and pulled his shirt out of his shorts. Her hands reached under his shirt and she moved them up to feel his muscular chest. She could feel soft hairs and wanted to feel more. Carl pulled back.

"Rena," he said, and in one scoop, picked her up into his arms. He started up the stairs. "Where is your room?" he asked gruffly.

Rena pointed to the door to the side of the stairs. Carl moved quickly, opened the door, and gently laid her on her bed. He quickly unbuttoned his shirt, took it off and threw it to the other side of the bed. He unbuttoned the top of his shorts and moved on top of Rena. He kissed her again and moved his hand expertly up her dress. His hand cupped in between her legs and Rena arched her back. He squeezed gently with his hand, and Rena felt blood rush to the area. *Oh my god*, she thought. *I want him so badly.* Carl moved back, took Rena's hands, and sat her up. He reached behind her dress and undid her zipper. Rena shivered in anticipation. Carl quickly picked up the bottom of her dress and pulled it up over her head. He gasped when he saw her half naked.

God Rena," he said.

He bent down to kiss her and expertly unclipped her bra and removed it. His mouth moved to her nipples, licking, teasing, and pulling. Rena moaned. He gently laid her back down and moved himself slowly down her body to her panties. He kissed her panties, then grasped the sides and moved them down her legs and off her body.

"Oh Rena," he said, sitting up and admiring her. "You are so beautiful."

Rena looked up at him. She had never experienced such passion before. Her body ached to feel his touch and the throbbing underneath his shorts was driving her mad.

"Come here," she said, trying to pull him down on top of her.

"Patience" Carl said with a small smile.

He quickly took off his shorts and Rena could see even more clearly his erection poking out from underneath his boxers. Carl kissed her again and then moved his head between her legs.

Rena couldn't believe it. In all her life, she had never felt this. Sure, she had had lovers, but she had never felt so sexy, so desirable, and so *needy*. She needed him inside her; she *wanted* him. Carl's mouth moved down from Rena's belly button softly kissing her every curve, and she thought she was going to lose it. How, she wasn't sure, but this was not normal. She felt supernatural and what was going on with her body was out of this world. She could feel Carl's breath between her legs and she was desperate, aching for his tongue.

"Carl, please," she begged.

Carl let out a groan and plunged his tongue into her sweetness. His tongue tickled, caressed and stroked her and Rena could feel the pleasure and pressure between her legs. She was going crazy with desire. The pressure mounted between her legs and she could feel herself reaching a plateau.

"Oh, Oh. Oh" She was shaking uncontrollably… *this is so good…*

Carl increased the pressure with his tongue and Rena started to shake. She could hear herself moaning, and felt on the precipice of release. Her body reacted and a gush of fluid dripped in between her legs.

"Oh, OOOOOOOOOOOOh," she cried out.

Her whole body enveloped with pleasure. Carl moved up her body, looked into her eyes, and plunged his tongue into her mouth. Rena grasped the sides of his boxers and pulled them down over his erection. He was hard and beautiful. She reached down with her hand to stroke him and he groaned.

"Let me do something for you" she said, and pushed him over onto his back.

She sat on his thighs and teased his erection with her hands. Then she knelt down and took him in her mouth. She could feel him shudder as she teased him with her tongue and gently move him in and out of her mouth. He was groaning and moving. He grasped her under her armpits and pulled her up until she was facing him.

"Rena!" he said. "You are too good at that, but we will talk about that later," he said and quickly moved her under him.

He leaned over her and kissed her gently. Then his kisses became more intense and Rena felt him move her legs apart with his. She felt his erection against her moistness and then he entered her.

Rena felt a bit of shock and tensed. Carl stopped.

"Geeze Rena, how long has it been? Why didn't you tell me?" he asked looking at her.

"It's okay," she said surprised at the initial feeling of pain. She hadn't had a lover since Jarod so it wasn't surprising that she had tightened up a bit. Carl started kissing her neck.

"Are you okay Rena?" "I'm sorry, I hope I wasn't too rough."

"No," she said, "It's been awhile, its okay."

Carl kept kissing her slowly, caressing her breasts. Rena began to feel the heat creep back into her body, and between her legs. She could feel the inside of her body begin to relax around him. As if on cue, Carl started to move slowly in and out of her. Rena moved to match him and felt him penetrate her further. The initial pain was gone, and Rena felt the friction of his erection moving inside her. Carl continued to move slowly and Rena started to feel her body react and want more. She wanted him to move, wanted him to move faster. As if he sensed her desire Carl started increased his movement. She could hear him moan and hear the sound of him mixing with her juices. She started to feel intense pressure, "Oh my god, oh...Oh," she cried out as she moved towards the edge. Carl plunged into her deeper and she could feel his breath beside her face. He kissed her and moved his tongue into her mouth as her body shuddered and released. She could hear her primal cries and hear him moan and against her. With one last plunge, she felt his body shudder and release and heard him cry out.

"God, Rena, I love you."

***

He relaxed on top of her. His breath was ragged and he could feel his heart beating a mile a minute. What had happened? He wasn't sure but this was the best time he had had in his life. She was soft and relaxed beneath him and he could feel her breath slowing down. He lifted up, kissed her on the mouth, and then moved off to the side. Rena smiled at him. They looked into each other's eyes for a bit. Rena spoke first.

"I don't know about you, but that was so good for me," she said with a sweet smile.

Carl grunted and pulled her close against him. He kissed her deeply and looked into her eyes. "That was good for me too Rena," he said. "I would really like to go again but my old body needs to rest for a bit."

Rena laughed. "That's okay I will take a raincheck," she said smiling and pulled away from him.

"Where are you going?" Carl said and pulled Rena close to him to spoon her. "This is the best part," he said holding her tight and kissing her neck. He could feel her relax in his arms.

"Yes it is," she said taking a deep breath and closing her eyes.

CHAPTER 16

They had quickie as he called it. Then he pulled away from her and played a game on his phone. He didn't look at her. She asked him if he wanted to cuddle. He told her there was not time, as he had to be up early the morning. Then he put his phone away and turned away from her.

She woke up and stretched reaching out to the pillow beside her. She sighed. She felt more relaxed than she had been in ages. She stretched out her arms and felt the empty pillow beside her. She felt like she should remember something. Oh. The realization hit her. She looked on the other side of the bed and noticed that Carl was gone. She was not sure how she should feel about that. Her body still recalled their lovemaking. Carl had been true to his promise and had given her a raincheck in the middle of the night. It had been great. Rena couldn't remember the last time someone had touched her, all over. She wasn't even sure it had ever happened before. But he was gone now and she was disappointed. She had hoped that this would have been more than a one-night affair. What was it he had said last night? Her brain was foggy, still on a high from the lovemaking. She snuggled deeper into the bed. She guessed she should get up, but sigh, she was going to wait a little bit.

Half an hour later she woke up, startled. She heard clanging and voices from downstairs. What was going on? Rena quickly got up, still naked and slipped on a robe. She was about to walk out of the bedroom when Carl walked in.

"Good morning beautiful," he said and pulled her towards him. His mouth rested on hers and he kissed her soundly.

"Hmmm," said Rena, "I thought you had left," she said.

"Just went to get breakfast sweetie," Carl said kissing her again. "Ugh, Rena, you feel so good," he said hugging her close.

Rena laughed, "Are you sure you want breakfast?

Carl smiled, "Yes, but definitely up for a *coffee* later," he teased.

Rena giggled. "Okay, let's go eat right now then," she said and pushed ahead of him out the bedroom door.

"Wait," Carl said catching her arm.

"What's up?" Rena said as Carl pulled her back into the bedroom. "Coffee time now?" she laughed.

Carl sighed, "I would love that Rena, but we have a guest and you can't go downstairs like that," he said.

"Like what?" she demanded.

"Tousled hair and looking like you were ravished the night before," he said eyes twinkling.

Rena looked in the mirror on the dresser. She *did* look like she had had quite the night. She giggled and then turned remembering Carl had mentioned a guest.

"Who's here?" she asked.

"Zio Augusto, said Carl, "so get some clothes on and brush your hair," he said grinning as the left the room.

Rena quickly jumped in the shower and got dressed. She looked at herself in the dresser mirror before leaving the bedroom. She was surprised at how relaxed she looked, and at the big smile grinning back at her. She felt great. She went down the stairs towards the kitchen. She could hear Carl talking to Zio Augusto in Italian and could smell something delicious. Her stomach growled. She got to the kitchen and Zio Augusto spotted her right away.

"Buongiorno Bellezza," he said getting up and planting a kiss on each of her cheeks.

"Bounjourno," Rena echoed.

Zio Augusto continued in a spatter of Italian and Rena nodded politely. Carl turned around from the stove and grinned. He said something to Zio Augusto and Zio Augusto started to laugh. It was a catchy loud laugh and Rena found herself amused and laughed along.

"I'm a sorry, bella, I no, I forget you no speak Italiano," he said slowly.

Rena laughed. "That's okay, I really should learn."

Zio Augusto beamed. "Si, Si," he said and continued in Italian.

"Rena, you might have wished you didn't say that," Carl teased putting plates of French toast, cheese and fruit on the table. He went back to counter and brought back two cups of espresso and a mug for Rena.

"Here Rena, just for you," Carl said putting the mug down in front of her plate.

Rena took the mug and brought it to her lips fully expecting a mug of tea, and was surprised. "Oooh coffee," she exclaimed taking a bigger sip this time.

"Just the way you like it," said Carl with a wink.

Rena felt her face go red and hoped that Zio Augusto didn't notice. It was a bit embarrassing having him here. She was sure he knew that Carl didn't arrive back at his place last night. Even though they were both adults, and neither of them was attached, Rena didn't want Anna's Uncle Augusto thinking any less of her.

They finished their breakfast and Rena cleaned up the dishes while Zio Augusto and Carl examined Anna and Simon's garden. Rena could see them out of the kitchen windows hands gesturing, measuring with their feet and nodding in agreement. She was curious what they were up to and wondered if this was going to be something Anna wanted. Carl wandered back into the house leaving Zio Augusto outside examining the backyard.

"What's he up to?" Rena asked when Carl came into the kitchen.

"He wants to build Simon a vegetable garden."

"That's a great idea," said Rena knowing that Anna would approve of anything that made Simon happy. "I think he would love that," she said, thinking that any chef would love his own vegetable garden.

"Yah," said Carl. "Apparently he's wanted to do this for

a while but has had a lot of trips to go on." "Zio Augusto wants to get started on it so that it will be ready when Simon and Anna return. He wants me to help him today," Carl said looking at Rena apologetically. He moved toward her putting his arm around her waist and pulling her toward him. "I really wanted to spend more time with you," he said.

"Is Falcone going to help too?" Rena asked wondering how Falcone had wormed himself out of helping out.

"No, he's still in Rome. He met someone there, I think," said Carl with a grin. "He'll be back in a couple of days though, Carl said.

"I wonder what I will do today then," said Rena thinking of a return trip to the shops.

"Actually Rena, Uncle Augusto has plans for you too," he said somewhat ashamedly.

"I don't know anything about gardening really, but I guess I could try," said Rena shrugging her shoulders.

Ah, yah, that's the thing Rena," said Carl looking somewhat guilty.

"What?" said Rena starting to feel a bit annoyed.

"You are going to help his wife get ready for the town festa," Carl said, and walked out of the kitchen before Rena could respond.

***

Rena wiped the windowsill in the church. After Carl had walked out of the kitchen, Zio Augusto had come in and instructed Rena in broken English to go to the church and ask for Zia Teresa. Rena had walked up the hill to the

95

church not knowing what to expect. She was disappointed that she could not spend more time with Carl, but had to agree that it was better that she at least had something to do to take her mind off him. When she arrived at the church, there were several women outside all chatting excitedly gesturing and seemingly arguing about something. A short stout woman with big brown eyes and a bright smile greeted Rena. Rena would have known Falcone's mom anywhere. She could see the resemblance in the mouth and dimples. Falcone's mom greeted her with a kiss on each cheek and introduced Rena to each of the women who also greeted her with kisses. After the greetings were over, Zia Teresa gestured to her to come into the church with the other women. Rena looked in awe again at the church she had been in just a few days before. With a smile, Zia Teresa grabbed Rena's arm, gave her a bucket and a cloth, and motioned to her to clean the windowsills.

As Rena started cleaning, she watched as the women lowered the statue of Our Lady of Ascension from a nook high up in the wall above the old altar. She had found out earlier that the statue weighed 264 pounds and was taken down once a year for the festa, but was surprised that the small group of women was who was doing it. Rena looked around; other women were cleaning the pews and adding flowers to the windowsills that Rena had cleaned. A few minutes later, a huge bouquet of flowers was added to the ledge where the statue had been, and two huge bouquets now stood in front of the statue on the old altar. Rena was surprised at how quickly these women worked and how efficiently they did everything.

She spent the whole day in the church cleaning and helping until her muscles ached. At 8pm, the chores had ended, and Falcone's mom took Rena to her home for 'pranzo'. Carl and Zio Augusto were already there and they enjoyed a meal of homemade bread with ham, sausage, white wine and salad. At 10pm, after chatting and gesturing to get ideas across, Rena yawned. It had been a long day and she had not had much sleep the night before. Carl noticed and told Rena he would take her home. She thanked Falcone's parents and got kissed on the each cheek twice, and followed Carl to the Fiat. Carl opened the door for her and she tumbled in.

"I'm exhausted!" she said, leaning back on the passenger seat and closing her eyes.

Carl reached over and quickly kissed her on the mouth. "Tell me about it," he said. "Zio Augusto kept me working all day in that hot sun, I'm exhausted as well." He started the Fiat and drove out of the laneway.

When they arrived at Anna's house, Carl got out of the Fiat and opened the door for Rena. He helped Rena out and leaned her back against the car. His mouth quickly found hers and he cajoled her lips open with his tongue. His kiss was gentle and comforting. Rena wished she didn't feel so tired.

"Rena, I have to go back," Carl said. "I don't want to tarnish your reputation," he said, smiling and kissing her again.

Rena felt the heat start to rise in her body but felt too tired to pursue it. "Yes," she said. "I don't want Anna to be embarrassed," she said.

"Meet me at the church tomorrow," Carl said. "We can go to a celebration in Bicarri."

"Sounds like a plan," said Rena smiling. Carl walked Rena to the door and kissed her again.

"Goodnight sweetheart."

"Goodnight Carl."

CHAPTER 17

Rena woke up bright and early the next morning. She was surprised how energetic she felt considering she had cleaned for hours the day before. She had a long shower, and afterwards lingered in the kitchen with a big slice of fresh bread with ricotta and a cup of tea. She looked at the meager supplies that were left in Anna's pantry and realized that she had to do some shopping. She would mention that to Carl today.

After cleaning up the breakfast dishes, Rena walked up the hill to attend the mass. The day didn't feel as hot as the one before, and Rena enjoyed the view of the mountains around her as she walked up the hill to the church. Other people from the town were walking up to the church as well and greeted Rena with a 'Buongiorno' and a smile. "It is nice to be a part of such a community," thought Rena. She could understand now why Anna had chosen this place for her and Simon to settle down. As she approached the top of the hill, Rena saw him. Standing against a stone fence near the church, he was wearing beige khakis and a cream top. Rena quickened her pace to meet him and saw his face light up with a smile when he saw her.

***

He had spotted her at the bottom of the hill. He would have spotted her anywhere. She was wearing a cute little flowery dress and her hair was flowing with the breeze. Carl couldn't take his eyes off her. The last two days had been like a dream and he didn't want to wake up from it. To say he had never experienced what he had with Rena was an understatement. Their night of lovemaking had thrown him for a loop. He hadn't expected to feel what he did, and definitely had not expected his body and hers to mesh so well. He couldn't remember having multiple orgasms since his twenties, and had been a little surprised and very pleased when he had. But it had exhausted him. He was definitely going to have to keep up his fitness level to match her. But she had been a dream. And he had been shocked to discover how tight she was. But even more shocking was how she had pulled away from him afterwards. During lovemaking, she had been all in, but once it was done, she had moved away and had looked shocked when he wanted to hold her. He was beginning to believe that there had been more to that marriage of hers than she was letting on. It made his blood boil to think that her husband had maybe not shown her the affection he should have. She was a beautiful, sweet, loving woman and deserved the best. He only hoped that he would have the privilege to continue to deliver on that.

***

Rena reached the top of the hill and walked with a big smile to greet Carl. He was gorgeous and she desperately wanted to hold him but it was too public here. She greeted him and accepted the traditional cheek kisses from Carl. He gazed at her with his beautiful brown eyes and Rena thought she was going to melt right there. The church bells started chiming and Carl guided Rena into a pew at the back of the church. Several women that had been cleaning the day before with Rena greeted her with nods and a smile. The mass was less than an hour and afterwards Rena and Carl walked out with the throng onto the front gardens of the church. Carl grabbed Rena's hand and started walking with her to Falcone's Fiat.

"Zia Teresa invited you to have lunch at the house today," he said, " I thought we could do that and then go to Bicarri for the Festival of the Old Village , and maybe afterwards enjoy a *coffee* together."

He looked at her searchingly as if he wasn't sure she would find this a good idea. Rena laughed inwardly to herself. She would go anywhere with him. Even up a high mountain. And *coffee*, well, that word meant a lot more than it used to. She turned to look at him with a smile. "Sounds great," she said.

They arrived at Falcone's parents' house and were greeted by several of Falcone's relatives that were also there for lunch. After being introduced to everyone, they sat down at a huge table in the garden for a meal of roast chicken, fried potatoes with parsley and oregano, and trifle for desert. The conversation was lively and a mix of Italian and English and Rena found herself enjoying it immensely.

After the meal was completed, Carl got up and said a few words in Italian and he and Rena said their goodbyes. They thanked Zio Augusto and Zia Teresa for lunch, promised to come again, and then walked to the Fiat. Carl let Rena into the car, and then excused himself for a moment and came back out with a knapsack and a grin on his face. He put the backpack in the trunk and got into the driver seat. He turned and grinned at Rena.

"You look like the cat that ate the canary," said Rena amused.

"Later," Carl said looking at her seductively.

Rena felt a warmth gather in between her legs. *He has such an effect on me*, she thought. "What's in the bag?" she asked him.

"A change of clothes and my toothbrush," he said, backing out of the laneway.

"I thought you were worried about my reputation," Rena said grinning.

Carl stopped the car and looked at Rena intently. "There is no way I am going to let anyone keep me from spending another night with you," Carl said determinedly.

The drive to Bicarri went quickly as Rena and Carl chatted about the work Carl was doing with the police in Bicarri with Falcone. "I will have to go back there soon Rena," Carl said. Rena felt her heart sink a little bit. She knew that he would have to go back at some point but she had hoped it wasn't too soon, and didn't want her time with Carl to end.

"Will Falcone be back soon then?" she asked.

"Yes," Carl answered, "In a few days, and then we're expected back to train with a group of new recruits."

"Oh," said Rena, "I wish you didn't have to back, sorry if that sounds selfish," she said shyly.

"Not selfish at all," said Carl. "I would rather just spend time with you Rena, but I have to get back to work. We're not that far way sweetheart," he said turning off the roadway and stroking her hair with his right hand.

Rena felt like her heart would break. He was so kind to her, it was all a bit strange and foreign, and painful. She knew in her heart that this was good, and that she was worth loving. She had never felt that way with Jarod. Some piece of her, some piece deep down had opened up since she had met Carl. And she felt sad, sad that she hadn't realized that she had been worth loving before, and angry, angry at herself for letting Jarod's actions make her feel less than loveable for so long. She wiped a tear from her face and looked ahead hoping Carl wouldn't notice. But he did.

CHAPTER 18

"Rena, what's wrong?" Carl swerved the Fiat suddenly and parked at the side of the road.

"Damn," thought Rena, "He saw!"

"Rena, why are you crying?

Rena kept looking ahead. "It's nothing, really," said Rena tears welling up in her eyes.

"Rena, for petes sake look at me!" Carl demanded taking off his seatbelt and coaxing her chin to face him.

Rena looked at him.

"Rena, what's wrong, did I say something to upset you?' he asked.

Rena kept looking into his eyes.

"Rena, you know that this doesn't end here, in Italy right? You know that I fully intend for us to keep going in Toronto, you know that right?"

"He looks so upset and so worried about me," thought Rena.

"Rena, talk to me," Carl said his voice getting more demanding. "You want the same thing, don't you?" he asked looking a bit insecure.

Rena broke down and sobbed. She sobbed as though her heart would break and never mend. Carl undid her seatbelt and held her close to him. Rena held him tight and continued sobbing. When she felt like she could sob no more, she pulled away and looked at Carl. She had never seen someone look at her the way he was now.

"Rena," Carl wiped the tears away from her cheek, "Was this too soon? I'm so sorry if I pushed you into something you weren't ready for," he said gently.

"Oh my God," thought Rena, "he thinks this is his fault?" "No, Carl, no," she said shaking her head.

"Rena, you can trust me, what is it?"

Rena sighed and looked straight at Carl. "I'm not s-sad about Jarod," Rena said her voice shaking. "I'm not sad now, and I w-w-asn't s-sad when he died."

***

Carl was shocked. He had seen Rena wipe away a tear and he was worried that he had upset her in some way. But he hadn't expected this. He had known something was up with Rena's marriage. He just hadn't wanted to believe it. Couldn't believe it. Didn't want to believe it. And now, here she was, letting him know it wasn't all roses and sunshine and it made him feel angry. Angry with the husband she felt guilty for not grieving for. Carl slowly got out of the car and walked around to Rena's side. He opened the door, took her hand, and started walking with her into a meadow of yellow flowers. When they had walked about 20 feet from the road, Carl sat down on the grass and coaxed Rena down beside him. Carl looked at Rena and thought his heart would break. The tears were spilling down her cheeks and her eyes looked wide and sad. He didn't want to know it all, but he had to. He needed to know. "Rena, tell me, tell me everything," he said.

And she did. She told him everything. She told him about her hopes and dreams for her marriage. She told him about the great start on her honeymoon. She told him how it all changed right after, and how devastated she was. She told him that she never felt good enough in the marriage that she was afraid to be herself because Jarod would lose his temper or be dismissive, that she had lost herself, and that she was sad and angry. Angry with Jarod and angry with herself. She told him that she had been afraid to find a way out, and when Jarod had died, the way out had been presented to her so easily, and that she had been relieved. She told him that she was scared, scared to lose herself again. And she told him that she was happy, that he made her feel loved, and that she had never felt that way before. Carl held her in his arms, his heart bursting with compassion and love for her. He needed to let her know that she wasn't alone. He needed to let her know that he trusted her enough to let her into his past.

And then told her. He told her about his first marriage. How in love they had been. How excited they were to start their life together. He told her how they had wanted to start a family and how he had got sick, and found out he had got cancer. He told her how his wife had stuck by him while he underwent chemotherapy, how she had been there to wipe his face when he was sick, and hold his hand when he was scared. And then he told her how when he got well, his wife had left, and that he had been devastated. That he had other relationships soon after that were unhealthy and had not worked out and he had felt sad, alone, and unworthy of love. And then he took her into his arms, held her, and told her that his life started to turn around when he had forgiven his wife for leaving him. That he knew it must have taken a lot out of her to care for him. That they both had tried their best and sometimes things just didn't work out. That he had forgiven his wife and more importantly, that he had forgiven himself. And that it was all okay. They were all doing the best they could with what they knew, and nobody was to blame. He had let it go, and that had allowed him to live and to love again. And that had led him to her.

He held her close. The breeze was warm. It moved the flowers and grass in the fields and brushed Rena's face with a tender touch that comforted her. She sighed and leaned back in Carl's arms.

"Rena," Carl said and moved her away to turn to him. "Rena," he said stroking her cheek and putting his hands in her hair, "Rena, I love you." "You know that don't you?" he asked.

Rena smiled and held Carl's face with her hands. "Yes, I know, and I love you too Carl," she said leaning in for a kiss.

His mouth crushed hers and his tongue quickly explored her mouth sending exhilarating sensations in Rena's body. He reached around her waist, moved her closer to him, kissed her again, this time more gently, and moved to her the nape of her neck. Rena let out a little moan. Carl sighed and let out a laugh and kissed her again before pulling her away.

"We can't do this here," he said moving a tendril of her hair that covered her face.

"I know," said Rena smiling.

"I love you so much Rena, I have to tell you something," Carl said earnestly as his phone interrupted them. Carl grabbed his phone out of his back pocket and looked at it. "Crap," he said, and answered the phone.

CHAPTER 19

They arrived in Bicarri for the Old Village Festival an hour later after hurriedly getting back into the car after Carl answered the phone. They had plans to meet Carl's colleagues in Bicarri for the festival and were already over an hour late. They met the group in the Piazza and Rena smiled to herself, remembering the first time she had been here, and how she had met Carl that very day. It seemed like a lifetime ago, but it hadn't been that long. The group consisted of three of Carl's colleagues, two of which had their wives visiting from Toronto and one had a new Italian girlfriend in tow. They quickly exchanged pleasantries and one of them asked Rena how she was doing after the ordeal at the adventure park.

"Fine, but a little embarrassed," she said smiling sheepishly.

"Ah, don't be," said one of the men named Drake. "Carl loves to rescue the damsel in distress," he said chuckling.

"Ha-ha very funny," said Carl grinning.

Drake laughed and winked at Rena. "It's true," he

whispered loudly.

They all laughed and Carl took Rena's hand as they walked across the Piazza through the historic center of Bicarri.

As they walked through the town, they sampled local cheeses, pizza, cured meats and wine being offered outside cafes and vendors stalls. They admired sites along the way and then joined a guided tour through exhibitions of the art and history of the town in the Civic Tower and Town Hall Square. Rena thoroughly enjoyed soaking in the atmosphere and excitement all around her. After walking for a couple of hours, they sat down on a restaurant patio and ordered mouthwatering pizzas with more wine. They could hear a Celtic band start playing and Rena found it amusing to hear such a band in Italy. The music was catchy and Rena felt herself dancing in her seat. After the meal, they walked to another piazza and listened and danced to another band.

The music was still going strong at midnight and Rena reluctantly gave in when Carl said they should probably go. "I could stay and dance forever," Rena said her eyes shining brightly.

"Well you could," said Carl, "but I have plans for you tonight," he said with meaning.

Rena giggled, "On second thought, why are we still here?" she said and grabbed Carl's arm and pulled him towards where the Fiat was parked.

***

They arrived back at Anna's house just after two am. "Coffee?" Rena asked when they had got into the house.

Carl grinned. "Actually Rena, it's 2am, and I would

actually really like a coffee," he said mischievously.

Rena looked at him narrowing her eyes. "I can't tell if you are joking or not," she said.

Carl laughed and pulled her close. "Rena, I plan to keep you up most of the night, so I really need a coffee, really."

Fifteen minutes later Rena had the espresso ready and served the thick liquid with a lot of milk in big mugs. It still didn't taste quite like the coffee at home, but she was getting used to it. Carl sat across from her at Anna's kitchen table. He sipped his coffee and stared at Rena. If Rena could have described his look, it would have been something like she had read in a book before. Something like, *his smoldering look was undressing her with his eyes*. Rena stared back. There would have been a time, not too long ago where she would have thought she did not deserve him. But looking at him stare at her, this god-like stunning creature, she knew he was hers. Carl kept staring at Rena and then, suddenly, put down his cup.

"Forget the coffee," he said quickly moving to the other side of the table and scooping Rena up.

He took Rena slowly up the stairs to the bedroom all the while telling her that he was going to kiss every inch of her body. Rena shivered with delight.

"My goodness," she thought, *he hasn't even touched me and I am feeling it*.

Carl sat her down gently on the bed. He sat down beside her, put his hand through her hair, and gently kissed her. His kiss was gentle, demanding, and seductive. He teased Rena's lips open with his tongue and expertly moved his tongue in her mouth. His other hand cupped her breast and he squeezed gently and teased her nipple with his thumb. Rena moaned. He kissed her neck and started to unbutton her the front of her dress.

"I need to see you," he said almost desperately and pulled her dress up over her head.

He gasped looking at her lacey bra and panties. He tossed her dress aside and kissed her neck again. He lowered her bra straps on either side and quickly slipped her bra down. He undid her clasp and the bra slipped away. He gently cupped each breast and brought his head down each nipple. His tongue teased and pulled at her nipples. Rena felt the hot wetness between her legs begin to moisten her panties. His hand slid down the side of her body to her hip. His fingers found their way under her panties to her moistness. He teased her clitoris with his finger while his mouth found hers again. Rena started to shake and could feel the wetness of her on his fingers. He inserted a finger inside her and stroked her gently. Rena arched her back and her hands quickly found his pants and started to undo them.

"Wait," Carl stopped her. "Wait," he said.

He gently laid her down on the bed and moved to the edge of the bed. He easily slipped off his shirt to show his muscular chest.

God I love that chest, Rena thought. "Please Carl," she begged.

Carl gave her a small smile, "wait, I need to kiss every inch of you first," he said.

He moved down to the side of her bed and started to massage her foot. Then he did what Rena could never have imagined. He took Rena's foot and starting sucking on her toes.

"Oh," Rena said in surprise.

"You don't like this?" Carl said looking at her intensely.

"No, I mean, I don't know, nobody has ever done this to me before," she said.

Carl smiled and started sucking and licking her toes. Rena could feel the heat rise in the body. She moaned again.

"Are you still not sure if you like this?" Carl asked huskily.

"Oh, I like it," Rena said breathlessly.

Carl continued with her other foot and then starting kissing the inside of her ankle. He started moving up her leg and Rena thought she would die from desire as she could feel the softness of his lips on her skin.

"Oh, please," she begged.

Carl continued to kiss her and got to the moist sweetness between her legs. His tongue found her clitoris and he expertly teased, licked and sucked her.

"Oh my God," cried Rena.

"Hang on, wait," said Carl with ragged breath.

Rena didn't want him to stop. This was driving her crazy. She didn't think she could hold on. He breathed on her and then moved up to her belly button kissing every inch of her. He came again to her breasts and when his tongue touched her nipples, she thought she was going to die of deliriousness.

"Uh," Rena," Carl said breathlessly, I don't think I can hold on."

"Don't, please," begged Rena.

With a grunt, Carl entered her and slowly starting moving his body against hers. Rena quickly matched his movement. Her body had never felt this on fire. He increased his speed and Rena's body matched his urgency. She could hear him panting and moaning near her ear. My god she loved this man.

"Rena," he cried out.

"Yes, yes!" she said, as her body shuddered and released.

She could feel his climax match her own and felt his body shudder against hers. "My god, I love you," he said staring into her eyes as he lay down to catch his breath on top of her.

CHAPTER 20

The sound woke him up with a start. Did he hear gunshots? He heard the sound again and quickly jumped out of the bed and stood beside the window looking out. Rena sat up in bed rubbing her eyes to adjust to the morning sun.

"What is that noise?" she asked looking at Carl's naked body standing beside the window.

"It's fireworks!" exclaimed Carl. "I thought it was gunshots," he said turning to look at Rena sheepishly.

"Fireworks?"

Rena quickly jumped out of bed grabbing the sheet to wrap around her. She went to the window and looked out. Fireworks of gold, red, silver and green were shooting into the sky. Carl held Rena close in front of him. He had never seen fireworks in daylight before. "This is phenomenal," he thought. Phenomenal and a little early, what time was it anyway? He and Rena had had a perfect day and even better night. He wasn't sure what time they had finally fallen asleep, but he knew it had been the wee hours of the morning, and somehow this didn't feel like many hours had passed.

"It's so beautiful," Rena said directing his thoughts back to the fireworks.

"Yes, it is," he said kissing her head and holding her closer.

"I wonder why they are shooting off fireworks?" Rena asked.

"Not sure – oh wait," Carl said the realization dawning on him. "Today is the festa."

"Oh," said Rena, "Neat that they do fireworks in the morning, what time is it?"

Carl let her go and went the side table to look at his phone. "It's 7am, and look, Zio Augusto has already called and left a message."

They went back to bed cuddling close together and woke up an hour and half later when Carl's phone rang. Carl grabbed the phone and looked at it. It was Zio Augusto again. "It must be something urgent," he thought answering the phone.

***

Rena heard Carl talking on the phone in Italian and rolled over to the other side of the bed. She was tired and she wanted to sleep. She felt Carl nudge her.

"Rena, sleepy head, we have to get up," Carl said.

Rena mumbled something unintelligible.

"I'm going to jump in the shower," Carl said. "You have ten minutes."

Ten minutes later, as promised Carl shook Rena awake and planted a kiss on her mouth. "What is it?" asked Rena all sleepy eyed.

"It's the festa Rena, and Falcone's parents are meeting us for the procession."

"We can't sleep in?" Rena asked.

Carl chuckled to himself. She looked so sleepy and distraught about getting up that he just wanted to take her into his arms then and there. But he knew that wouldn't work. If he did that, they wouldn't be going anywhere.

"Com'on, shower time," he said picking her up off the bed and bringing her into the bathroom.

Half an hour later, Rena and Carl left Anna's house and went to the main street to find Falcone's parents. They saw them near the hill to the church and hurried up the street to meet them. Zio Augusto was all smiles and swiftly planted his kisses on Rena's cheeks. His wife Teresa was next. They introduced Carl and Rena to some of their friends and more kissing ensued. "I've never been kissed by so many strangers in such a short amount of time," thought Rena. She giggled. The thought made her laugh.

"What's so funny? whispered Carl into her ear behind her.

"I was just thinking that I have never been kissed by so many strangers in such a short time," she said turning to look at him with a big grin.

"Hmm," said Carl giving her a kiss on each cheek.

"What was that for?" asked Rena.

"I want to be the last kiss you remember," Carl said with a smile.

The crowd started to move towards the bottom of the street and Rena and Carl moved with them. They could hear and see a marching band playing various instruments coming up the street. Behind the band, they saw the statue of Our Lady being lifted by eight men following the band up the street. Scores of people walked behind the statue as the procession made its way to the church. Rena saw people leave the crowds at various points along the way and pin money on a ribbon that was on the bottom of the statue of Our Lady.

"What are they pinning the money for?" asked Rena.

Zio Augusto answered in Italian to Carl. "It's a way to pay for the festa," said Carl.

"Oh, kind of like the other party," Rena said, "What a neat idea," she said thoroughly enjoying the site before her.

They followed the procession up the hill and stood with the crowds outside the church. A tall man started rushing for the church and everybody clapped.

Zio Augusto turned to Rena and said, "Il vescovo, Beeshop," he said proudly.

"Oh," said Rena nodding.

She looked questioningly at Carl who mouthed, "Bishop." "

Si, si," said Rena smiling at Zio Augusto.

They followed the other people of the town into the church for mass. The bishop said the mass and Rena looked around at all the people praying. It was wonderful. Carl took her hand in his and Rena smiled. *My life has changed so much*, she thought. She felt grateful and blessed.

***

   After the mass Rena and Carl followed Uncle Augusto and Zia Teresa down the road to the park, where a group of women in colourful costumes were singing and dancing on a stage. The music was upbeat and catchy and Rena found herself clapping to them as they danced. The park was decorated with bright lights and rows of bleachers full of people. There was a ferris wheel, a merry-go-round with horses and other animals, and a ride with swings that moved around in a circle suspended from the top. Children were laughing and running around and dancing to the music, and adults were clapping and drinking soft drinks and coffee.

   Rena and Carl followed Uncle Augusto and Zia Teresa to one of the stands to watch the show. The dancing group twirled around their beautiful costumes creating a kaleidoscope of colour. Rena kept up clapping with the beat and enthusiastically clapped when they finished. After the dancing group went off stage, another group of five singers went on stage and sang and played instruments. Carl leaned over to Zio Augusto and said something and then grabbed Rena's hand and took her on a walk through the park. "I had to have some time alone with you Rena," he said smiling at her.

   Rena looked up at him at beamed. Carl felt his heart jump at her smile. Last night had been the second most incredible night of his life and it was all due to her. She was beautiful and sexy, and sweet and he was in love with her. Rena reached up and kissed Carl on the mouth, lingering. "Rena, we are going to make a spectacle of ourselves," he said laughing.

"I don't care," she said and kissed him again.

Three hours later after wandering around the park and enjoying the entertainment, they found themselves at Zio Augusto and Zia Teresa's house for another meal. Rena thought it looked like half the towns people had come this time. Some of the performers from earlier in the day were also there. They feasted on pasta, bread, salads, meat and wine. They chatted amicably with others at the table as some of the town's people spoke English. Two hours later the meal winded down and as some of the people were beginning to leave, Carl whispered to Rena, "Let's go." They said their goodbyes to Zio Augusto and Zia Teresa, thanked them, and promised to meet them again the next day. They started walking back into town and some of the town's people that had been with them for dinner offered them a lift, but they declined enjoying the warm night and their time together.

This was a great day," said Rena as they approached the park again.

"Yes, it was, and it still seems to be going on," Carl said as they heard music and could see lights and a crowd in the park. "Want to go see?" Carl asked turning to Rena.

"Sure, why not?" she said.

They approached the park and heard a band playing soft music. Couples and children were dancing to the music in front of the stage that was lit up with stringed lights. Carl moved Rena toward the stage, turned her face him, held her close, and started moving to the music. They danced with the couples in the park and Rena could feel the tears stinging in her eyes.

"Rena, what's wrong beautiful," Carl asked noticing her shining eyes.

"I am so happy," Rena gasped, "This is just so beautiful," she said with emotion.

"I'm happy too," said Carl looking into Rena's eyes. "Rena, you make me feel alive again," he said giving her a slow kiss.

"I love you Carl," she said pulling him closer to her.

***

She told him she wanted to do more with him. He usually came home from work, changed, grabbed a glass of wine, and disappeared into the basement. She wouldn't see him for hours. This time she followed him down the stairs. She asked him if he would take ballroom dancing with her, he said no, he didn't like dancing. She asked him if he would join a running group with her, he said no, he didn't like running. She asked him what he would do with her. Skydiving, he said. She reminded him she was afraid of heights. He looked at her, shrugged his shoulders, and then walked away.

"Of course I'll dance with you." Rena woke up with a start her eyes fighting to stay closed. She could hear the fireworks going off again but wasn't in the mood to get up. She felt Carl move close and wrap his arms around her. "Of course I'll dance with you Rena," he said, "Go back to sleep."

CHAPTER 21

Rena woke up. She wiggled in the bed and leaned over to touch Carl. He wasn't there. She had hoped to wake up in his arms. That had never happened for her before. Not with Jarod, and not with any of her other lovers. She relaxed further into the bed. She was having a wonderful time and felt loved for the first time in years. She felt blessed. Ten minutes later, she noticed the smell of fresh brewed coffee and bacon wafting into the room. Her stomach growled. Rena jumped up, put on her robe, and sauntered down the stairs. When she got into the kitchen, she saw a beautiful bouquet of pink roses on the table and Carl busily cooking at the stove. Rena walked up to the table and inhaled the smell of the roses. There were at least two dozen of them and the bouquet was one of the most beautiful she had ever seen. The smell was glorious and she inhaled deeply. Carl was busy at the stove and didn't notice her. Rena tiptoed up behind him and wrapped her arms around his waist. Carl jumped.

"Woah," he said.

Rena laughed. "Did I scare you?" she asked laughter in

her voice.

Carl flipped a piece of French toast and turned around to pull her close to him. He kissed her soundly. "Good morning beautiful," he said.

"Good morning," Rena said, "Thanks for the flowers."

"They reminded me of you," said Carl kissing her again.

Rena looked around. Carl had been busy. There was French toast cooking in the pan, bacon on the griddle and coffee percolating on the stove. "You've been busy," she said, "But where did you get all the food?" she asked surprised.

Carl laughed. "I went shopping this morning," he said, "You had nothing here, didn't you know you were running low on food?"

"Actually I did," said Rena, "but I guess I forgot," she said giggling. "Guess it is true about losing weight when you were in love," she surmised. She was so in love she forgot about food!

They ate their breakfast unhurriedly and cleaned up slowly. They were to meet Zio Augusto and Zia Teresa for another procession, but this time Carl had made excuses so they could skip the mass. Rena was glad. She considered herself a good Catholic, but mass more than once a week was too much for her. They showered together taking their time lathering each other up, kissing, and touching, and making love. They took turns drying each other off and then got dressed and met Zio Augusto and Zia Teresa for the procession. They met again at the side of the road and Rena greeted Falcone's parents with the traditional kiss. Carl put his arm around Rena as they watched the procession move up the street. This time it was for St. Rocco and four girls were carrying the statue.

Rena found out from Carl that the statue weighed 68 pounds and was taken from village to village. A couple of men followed the statue carrying a table.

"If anyone wants to make a donation, they place the table in front of their house," Carl said to Rena. "Then they put the statue on the table and the people can pin money onto the ribbon around the statue," he pointed out.

They followed the procession up to the church and then said their goodbyes as Zio Augusto and Zia Teresa entered the church. The church was packed and speakers had been set up outside for the extra crowds to listen to the mass. Rena and Carl quickly darted through the crowd and made their way back down the hill. Carl took Rena's hand and they walked through the town listening to the mass as they went along. A few shops were open and they greeted the storekeepers as they passed by. Carl ducked into a café, bought two cappuccinos and brought them out to the street. The found a bench and sat and enjoyed the drinks watching the towns people mill about.

"Rena, I am going to miss this when I go back to Bicarri," Carl said breaking the silence.

"Yes, me too," said Rena, "Do you know when you are going?" she asked.

"Falcone called me this morning. He's coming back this evening and we will go back in a couple of days' time."

Rena felt the disappointment rise in her stomach.

"Rena," Carl turned to look at her earnestly. "We can still meet on weekends, it's not too far away, I can rent a car."

"I'm glad you said that," said Rena smiling starting to feel a little better. "I was worried that you weren't going to have time to see me," she said.

"I will always make time for you," Carl said seriously kissing her on the forehead.

He put his arm around her and they sat in comfortable silence watching life go by on the street. Rena yawned. "Carl, I'm exhausted, I want to go back to bed," she said resting her head on his shoulder.

"I was hoping you'd say that," said Carl jumping up from the bench and hurrying Rena with him down the street.

***

Rena and Carl spent the rest of day in bed, sleeping, making love and coming up for air occasionally for the odd snack. Carl couldn't believe that Rena's husband hadn't wanted to touch her, make love to her. He had never felt skin so soft, and Rena was a thoughtful, adventurous lover. It stunned him to think that any man would ignore this treasure. To him she was the answer to his prayers. They had spent some time talking, while Carl's body took time to recover between lovemaking, about their hopes and dreams for the future, and what they would do once they were both in Toronto. They decided that neither of them wanted this to end and they were going to see each other in Toronto and go from there. Carl was going to help Rena figure out what work she wanted to do. Things were going to work; they both wanted them to.

Carl snuggled closer to Rena. Something was niggling at the back of his mind, disturbing his peacefulness. He felt like he had forgotten something, something important. He shook his head. He didn't want anything to ruin the last few days he had before he went back to Bicarri. He put his arms around her sleeping form and spooned her. He wanted to be there holding her when she woke up in the morning.

CHAPTER 22

The sex was always fast, and mostly only oral sex. He didn't like much touching. He aroused quickly, and got off quickly. He never wanted to cuddle afterwards. She always felt sad and alone afterwards.

He woke up before her. He could hear her soft breathing and feel the movement of her chest going up and down. She smelled sweet and felt warm. He snuggled closer to her and kissed her neck. It was nice waking up next to her. He could get used to this. Rena moved, mumbled, and then was still. He could hear her breathing slow down and could tell she had fallen back asleep. He held her closer. He hadn't expected any of this to happen. Italy was supposed to be a time for him to get embroiled in work, work on his career, make a name for himself, and not fall in love. But it had happened without him realizing, and he did not regret it. It felt right. This was good. Rena started moving again. Carl kissed her neck and starting licking the inside of her ear. He breathed on her ear and heard her moan. She turned around in his arms to face him.

"Good morning," she said seductively.

Carl held her close. "Good morning my love," he said, feeling his heart pour out to hers.

Her eyelids were half closed, her hair was tousled and she looked sleepy, dazed, and so sexy. She leaned forward and kissed him on the mouth, moving her tongue inside his mouth. He kissed her back, deepening the kiss. She sucked in her breath and for a moment, he felt like he couldn't breathe. Then she kissed him again, softly, moving her mouth expertly against his. "My god, what is this?" he thought.

She hadn't kissed him like this before. His body was reacting to the kiss and he was hardening faster than he normally would. He moved to deepen the kiss even further, but Rena pushed him away. He was surprised. "What?" he exclaimed feeling a bit confused.

Rena rolled him over on to his back and held him down with her arms. She straddled him, her long blonde hair caressing his chest as she leaned forward to kiss him. "I am in charge," she said softly and kissed his lips again.

She moved down, kissed his neck, and started sucking and licking down to his nape. Carl couldn't believe it. His body was reacting as if he was a 25 year old, and he was shaking with desire and anticipation. What was she doing? He felt mesmerized, he felt like he couldn't move, he was under her spell and she was completely in control. Rena continued kissing him and started moving down from his neck with her kisses. Carl felt his body tighten as she planted kisses on his chest. She took a nipple in her mouth and teased it with her tongue, pulling, sucking, and then blowing her hot breath on it. He couldn't stand it. He was eager. He wanted to please her now, and *badly*. He tried to roll her over but she resisted.

"No," she said firmly and pushed him back down. "I am in charge baby," she said with such a sexy forcefulness that he almost lost it then and there.

He took a deep breath. He needed to hold on. She kissed him again and started to move down his chest planting tender kisses along the way. The farther she moved down, the harder he became. "Rena, Rena, what are you doing to me?" he gasped.

She giggled. "Loving you, just loving you. Relax." Rena moved down below his belly button. He tensed. He knew what was coming but was so aroused he was not sure he could hold on.

"Rena, wait," he said.

"No, Carl, relax," Rena said, "Just relax."

She moved down and caressed him gently with her hands. She held him gently, softly, massaging him. He could feel her breath on his erection. When she took him into her mouth, he gasped. "Rena, oh Rena', he moaned as she moved him in and out of her mouth. "Rena!" he tensed and grabbed her hips. She stopped him and moved his hands to his sides.

"Carl, hold on, I want to make love to you," she said.

She moved up his navel kissing him until she was straddled above where he wanted her most. She leaned forward and kissed him sensuously on the mouth. Carl gripped her hips again. "Rena!"

She smiled seductively at him and slowly lowered herself onto him. What happened next he could only describe as surreal and out of this world. He could see her above him writhing, moving, her hair falling onto her generous breasts, her hips curvaceous and moving with him. She was licking her lips and stroking her breasts and she moved expertly on his erection. He could see the sweat gleaming on her body and thought that this was the most beautiful image he had ever seen. Ever. His hips joined in her movement and as she quickened, he quickened with her. He could see her chest rising and falling quickly and knew that she was almost there. She started to cry out. It was primal, loud, sexy, and drove Carl to the edge. With one swift movement, he grabbed her hips and dove into her crying out.

"Rena, God!"

He felt her writhe on him and then cry out. Her body shuddered around him as she climaxed and his whole body reverberated; releasing the built up pressure he had inside her. She cried out one more time and then fell against him, her hair caressing his chest. He could feel her panting and trying to catch her breath against his chest. *There is only one way to describe this. Ecstasy. Pure ecstasy.*

He held her for a long time, kissing her every so often to remind her that he was still there. When they were both ready, they got up slowly and skipped to the shower. The warm water embraced their skin as they playfully soaped up each other's bodies. It was wonderful, comfortable, and safe. They rinsed each other off and let the water fall on them as they kissed. When they finally got out of the shower, Carl grabbed the towels hanging on the rack, wrapped Rena in a towel, held her close to him, and kissed her. They stared into each other's eyes for a bit. It was good. Carl sniffed the air. "Coffee," he said.

"*Coffee*?" asked Rena. "Actually I *smell* coffee," said Rena giggling. "It must be my subconscious or something."

Carl moved away from her and dried off quickly. "I smell it too," he said, "Someone is here."

***

They went downstairs slowly and somewhat sheepishly. They figured it was probably Zio Augusto making himself at home. They didn't need to feel this way, they were adults, but somehow Zio Augusto seemed like a father figure to Rena, and she didn't want him to disapprove. They got to the bottom of the stairs and walked to the kitchen door.

"Wait," Carl whispered pulling Rena back. They could hear voices in the kitchen. Carl let out a laugh.

"It's Falcone," he said turning to Rena, "He has keys?"

"No clue," said Rena following Carl through the kitchen doorway.

"Hey buddy," Carl moved towards Falcone sitting at the table in the kitchen. Falcone got up from the chair smiling,

"Hey buddy," he said patting Carl on the back before they both sat down.

Rena stopped at the door. A tall brunette woman with her back to Rena was at the stove cooking. She turned around. Rena got a start. "Anna!" she exclaimed and quickly rushed to go and hug her. Anna hugged her spatula in hand. "When did you get back?" Rena asked excitedly.

"Just last night," she said. "I thought I would cook you some breakfast. From the sounds of things you used up a lot of energy last night," she said grinning.

"Oh," said Rena somewhat embarrassed. "Was it that loud?" she asked walking with Anna towards the table and lowering her voice so Falcone couldn't hear.

"Yes," piped in Falcone. "In fact, you guys should really close the window, you're the talk of the town now," he said.

Rena and Carl laughed and then stopped. Anna and Falcone looked serious.

"Are you kidding me?" asked Carl.

Anna and Falcone burst out laughing. "No, n-no, not kidding," Anna said between peals of laughter.

Rena stared and them and then looked at Carl. He looked back at her and shrugged his shoulders. "Seriously guys," Rena spoke up. "Are you joking or not? I don't want to make things difficult for you here Anna," Rena said seriously. Anna turned to look at Rena, tears of laughter filling her eyes.

"Oh Rena," she said calming down. "It's wonderful" she beamed. "And it's true."

"It's great," Falcone said still laughing.

"I don't get it," said Rena.

"Neither do I," piped in Carl sounding a bit annoyed.

"Oh Rena," Anna said taking her hands with hers. "Nobody in this town talks about me anymore. Because they think you're *worse*!" she said breaking down and laughing again.

Rena was shocked. *Worse?* What had she done? Anna calmed herself down looking at both Rena and Carl.

"I'm not the stuck-up harlot who brought her English lover to their town anymore," she said, "Now they are talking about the floozy widow who is jumping into bed when she should be wearing black and mourning."

"What?" exclaimed Carl. "I don't want them talking like that about Rena."

"Too bad," said Falcone grinning. "They used to think I was the great womanizer, the worst of the bunch," he said his grin getting wider, "But you are much worse. Tainting the poor widow and putting her on a path of sinfulness. Ah, I *love it*," Falcone said wickedly breaking down into laughter again.

Rena and Carl looked at their friends. "Seriously," said Rena. She was starting to get annoyed. "So I can live for years with a husband who always ignored me and treated me like a piece of meat and the one time I have something real, and I am happy I am condemned for it?," she said angrily tears stinging her eyes.

Anna got up from her seat and put her arms around Rena. "No, you are *living* Rena. The gossiping does not matter. What matters is that you never told me how unhappy you were with Jarod. Rena, I could have helped you!"

"You were busy with Simon and everything you were going through Anna, I couldn't do that to you," Rena said loving her friend for being so compassionate.

"Rena," Anna said, "You deserve to be happy, you always did, so don't let the gossiping of anyone here ruin that for you. There are worse things that go on in this town, and I'm sorry, I didn't want to upset you, I thought you would find it funny," she said giving Rena a big hug.

"Well, it is *kind* of funny," Rena said letting out a quick giggle and wiping her tears. "I mean, people thinking that Carl is worse than Falcone, now that is funny!" she said giving Falcone a huge grin.

"That a girl," said Falcone his grin matching hers, "There's the Rena I know and love," he said.

"Ahem," Carl said clearing his throat.

"A little competition never hurt anybody," Falcone said addressing his friend and winking at Rena.

Carl smiled. "Good one Falcone," he said pulling Rena's chair toward him, putting his arm around her, and kissing her cheek.

"Okay, well let's eat," said Anna getting up from the table. "Coffee anyone?"

Rena and Carl looked at each other and grinned. "Yes, would love some *coffee*," Carl said turning to look at Rena.

"Yes, me too," said Rena grinning.

"Okay, four coffees coming up," said Anna walking over to the other side of the counter.

Rena watched Anna and then started and jumped up from the table. "Anna, you have a coffee machine?" she exclaimed looking at the machine sitting on the counter.

"Of course I do," said Anna, "how else did you think I made coffee?"

Rena turned to look at Carl. "I swear I couldn't find it," Carl said innocently holding up his hands in surrender.

"I keep it in this cupboard," said Anna opening the door above the counter. "How were you making coffee?" she asked.

"Hey, I think I did a good job with the espresso maker," Carl interrupted.

Anna laughed. "That's how you made Rena coffee?" she asked amused. "How funny," she said grinning.

CHAPTER 23

The four of them sat and ate a breakfast of frittata, fresh bread and coffee and chatted about Anna's time in Dubai and Falcone's new love whom he met picking up his parents at the airport in Rome. "It is nice to have Anna back," thought Rena. Even though she had had a super time with Carl, it was great to have a girlfriend to talk to. Nothing compared to late night chats about men with a girlfriend over a few glasses of wine. She wanted to tell Anna everything about Carl and what had happened between them. It was important for Rena that Anna know that this was not just a fling.

They finished breakfast and Carl announced that Anna had to come to the backyard. They all followed him out the door to the backyard. "Oh, a vegetable garden!" Anna exclaimed delightedly. "Simon will love this!" she said wrapping her arms around Carl and giving him a big kiss.

"Well, thank your uncle too Anna, it was his idea," said Carl grinning.

"Oh, my Zio is awesome!" Anna said running into the

kitchen to give Zio Augusto a call.

Rena walked after her intent on cleaning up the breakfast mess while Anna was on the phone. Falcone turned to Carl. "Hey buddy, we have to talk," he said.

Rena cleaned up the kitchen making a special note to remember where the coffee maker went, while Anna chatted excitedly on the phone with Zio Augusto. When Anna got off the phone, she sat down with Rena at the kitchen table. "More coffee?" she asked.

"Sure," said Rena, "I would love another cup, but let me make it."

Rena got up to make the coffee and Anna asked her if she had seen anything in Italy since she had been away. "Yes, Carl took me to Pompeii, and we went partway up Mount Vesuvius."

"Really? Rena how wonderful," Anna said looking at her friend lovingly.

Rena poured the coffees and sat down with Anna. "Yes, it has been a whirlwind since you've been away, but really good."

"It sure sounds like it, how's the- ?" The men coming back into the kitchen interrupted Anna.

Carl looked solemn, Falcone looked apologetic, and Rena felt her heart sink. "You have to go, don't you," she said looking at Carl. Carl sighed.

"Yes, we have to go back and set up for the next round of training. The other guys need our help since this group is a big one." He walked over to where Rena was sitting.

"Well that sucks," said Anna, "I was hoping we could all

hang out together for a bit."

"We can," said Falcone, "but in about a week. "We need to get this stuff organized and then we can come back for a couple of days before training begins."

Rena felt dejected. She knew that Carl would have to go back to work, he had warned her, but deep down she had hoped that it had been wrong, that it wouldn't be so soon. Carl stroked her cheek and looked so dejected that Rena laughed. "I'll be fine," she said kissing him quickly on the mouth.

"Not sure I'll be," Carl said looking into her eyes. "I will miss you Rena," he said with meaning.

"It's seven days, ten days max guys, and when training starts, there's nothing to stop you from seeing each other on the weekends," Falcone interjected.

"That's true," said Rena still looking at Carl.

He squeezed her hand. "We're leaving today after lunch Rena."

"Oh, now that really sucks," she said letting Carl pull her to him.

They said their goodbyes after lunch. Rena clung to Carl. "I love you Carl," she whispered as she kissed him goodbye. "I am going to miss you so much," she said.

"Not as much as I will miss you," he said staring deeply into her eyes. "I love you too Rena," he said kissing her and holding her close before reluctantly tearing himself away and getting into Falcone's Fiat.

"Bye ladies," Falcone yelled out as he turned the car to go down the laneway.

"See you in a couple of days beautiful," Carl yelled out of the window as Falcone's Fiat sped away.

Anna and Rena watched the Fiat fade into the distance. "Well, now that they're gone," said Anna, "I want all the nitty gritty details," she said grinning.

"I can do that," said Rena grinning and wriggling her eyebrows.

***

After a chat where the girls shared stories of their time apart, Anna stood up from the couch in the living room and stretched her arms. "I know the best thing for both of us missing our men," she said. "Let's go do some retail therapy!" she suggested. Rena laughed. Leave it to Anna to want to go shopping the day she was back in Italy. But she had to admit, it was a great idea, and she was missing her girly time.

The girls quickly got ready and went into town in Anna's Fiat to shop. They parked in a small spot on the street and then browsed in and out of the shops. Three hours later, both were laden with several parcels, tired and hungry. "Let's go to Grottaminarda," said Anna, "I know a great place to have a pizza."

"Oh, that sounds good," said Rena. Her stomach was growling and she was exhausted from the afternoon of shopping. They put their parcels in the back of Anna's fiat and then drove 20 minutes through winding roads to arrive at a Pizzaria in the heart of Grottaminarda. The pizzeria was busy inside, so they took and table outside on the patio and ordered some wine.

"Pizza with anchovies, tomato and fresh cheese?" suggested Anna looking up from the menu.

"Sure," said Rena thinking that sounded great.

Anna ordered the food and the girls sat and sipped their wine. They talked about Rena and Carl, and then chatted about Simon and the work he was doing in Dubai.

"When is he coming home?" asked Rena.

"Soon," said Anna. "He has two more weeks and then he is back for a while. After that I will go with him to Portugal for a vacation," she said.

"Nice," said Rena taking another sip of her wine. She could feel the wine affecting her more than usual. "Must be because I am hungry," she thought.

"Okay so now that I asked the nice stuff," said Anna, "I want to know the nitty gritty details of you and Carl," she said mischievously.

"Really, Anna?" giggled Rena feeling the wine on her empty stomach a bit more.

"Yes, really," said Anna leaning forward on the table. "You sounded like you were having a great time," she said. "Were you faking it or is he great in bed?" she asked grinning.

"Awesome," Rena said slyly as the pizza came to the table. She was glad she didn't have to say more. It was nice to keep the details just between her and Carl.

The girls each took a slice of pizza. Rena lifted it to her mouth and took a big bite. She was hungry as they hadn't eaten since lunch and the wine was really getting to her. Rena munched on the pizza.

"Great pizza isn't it?" said Anna taking another bite.

"Hmmm," Rena nodded chewing.

As she continued to chew, something didn't feel right. The pizza started to taste more and more salty and greasy. She normally loved pizza, but for some reason she couldn't stomach this one.

"Oh," Rena said as her stomach lurched. She quickly spit out her bite into a napkin.

"What's up, you don't like it?" Anna said.

"I don't know," said Rena, "my stomach does not like it for some reason. It tastes really salty."

"Could be the anchovies," Anna said. "Let me order you a Neapolitan. Just tomato and cheese," she said waving down their waiter.

Ten minutes later the second pizza came. Rena took a piece and smelled it. It smelled wonderful. She took a bite and could taste the fresh tomato, basil and cheese. It was wonderful.

"Better?" Anna asked.

"Much," said Rena as she took another bite.

The second bite was also great and Rena felt relieved. She took another sip of wine and laughed at Anna who was retelling a story about one of her adventures with Simon. Rena lifted her pizza slice to take a third bite, and her stomach lurched again. Rena could feel the pizza at the back of her throat and thought she might just throw up.

"Rena, are you okay?" Anna asked looking at her worriedly.

"I think I'm going to be sick," Rena said.

The ride home wasn't great with Rena having to ask Anna to stop a couple of times, each time, worried that she was going to be sick in the Fiat. But she wasn't. Her stomach was churning but nothing was happening. Nothing was coming out.

When they finally got to Anna's place, Anna set Rena up on the couch and made her a cup of ginger tea. After sipping the tea, Rena felt a bit better. She smiled at her friend who was looking at her intently. "I'm okay now Anna, thanks, the tea helped," she said reaching out to touch her friend's hand. Anna looked relieved.

"You looked so pale, I wasn't sure what was wrong," said Anna.

"Probably not enough sleep," said Rena. "Carl and I had some late nights and were woken up at 7am from fireworks a few times."

"Can I get you something to eat?" Anna asked, "Maybe some bread?"

"A piece of that fresh Italian bread would be great, but no butter, I don't want to risk it," Rena said.

"Sure," said Anna getting up to go to the kitchen.

Rena started to get up to follow her but Anna shooed her back down. "You relax, I'll be right back," she said. She came back a few minutes later and Rena munched hungrily on the bread. It seemed to go well with the tea and after half an hour Rena felt back to herself.

"How odd," she said to Anna. "It must have been the lack of sleep or maybe too much coffee, I dunno," she said.

"Hard to know," said Anna, "but I am happy you are

okay. I was thinking we could go to the beach tomorrow, you game?" she asked.

"Sure, that sounds good," said Rena relaxing into the sofa. "Maybe a nice quiet day at the beach is what I need," she said.

The girls spent the rest of the evening watching a competition show on television between Belgium, France, Italy, Portugal, and San Moreno. The show had crazy competitions with people sitting in pots on titer totters, catching yellow muck in bags, races in water floating on toy horses, and people flying through the air splashing paint on each other. Rena and Anna laughed and enjoyed each other's company. They both went to bed early tired from the days' events. Rena got into bed snuggling under the covers when her phone beeped on the side table. She reached over and looked at the message. "Hope you had a great day beautiful, love you, Carl." Rena texted back and then lay back on her pillow with a smile on her face.

CHAPTER 24

The next morning Rena woke up early. She and Anna were going to the beach today and she was looking forward to it. She got up out of the bed slowly noticing that her stomach wasn't as queasy as the night before, but still a little bit off. "A good bit of tea and bread will help," she thought. She took a quick shower, got into her bikini, added a pink and blue flowered sundress on top, and slipped on pink flip-flops. She packed her sun bag with lotion, a book, and a big hat and took off down the stairs to meet Anna. Anna was already up and in the kitchen when she there.

"Hey good morning," she said adding the last of a picnic lunch to a basket. "Feeling okay this morning?" Anna asked.

"Great," said Rena. There was no point to worry Anna about a bit of queasiness. They had a quick breakfast of tea, bread and cheese and then packed the Fiat to take the trip to Torre Mileto.

The roads to Torre Mileto were very windy and Rena felt

her stomach churn a bit as they wound up and down the mountain to get to the sea. "This is normal," she thought, "My stomach always reacts this way, so no need to worry."

They got to Torre Mileto an hour and a half later. The beach was packed with tourists and locals, and the girls searched around before finding a nice spot in the middle of the beach. Anna had packed a big umbrella and set it up providing them with some much-needed shade. The girls laid out their towels, put on their sun lotion, and then went to test out the water. Rena was delighted. The Adriatic Sea expanse was beautiful and scenic. Rena and Anna swam and enjoyed the water for a couple of hours and then spent the rest of the afternoon sun bathing and dipping back into the water whenever they got too hot. They enjoyed the picnic that Anna made, and Rena felt calm, as her stomach seemed to happily be back to normal. They packed up to leave at 7 pm, sandy, tanned, and tired.

On the way back to Ariano Irpino, they stopped in Foggia at a small restaurant and had a meal of rapini, eel, fruit and ice cream. Anna ordered coffee for both of them and they chatted about Anna's next trip with Simon. When the coffee came, Rena let out a small exclamation of surprise, as the coffee looked smooth and creamy. "It's espresso with steamed milk," Anna said. "Just in case your stomach decides to have a party again," she giggled.

Rena lifted the coffee and took a sip. The foamy milk of the coffee was a nice surprise and Rena enjoyed it. "It's going down great," she said. "Maybe it was just a short bug," she mused.

"Could be," said Anna, "just take it easy, you are probably not used to all the hot sun here."

Rena agreed. Toronto could be warm in the summer, but it was not as far south as Italy, and the sun was definitely stronger here.

The drive back to the town brought them again through the winding roads and up and down the mountains and Rena felt her stomach churn again. This time she was a bit more worried as the full meal and milky coffee made the churning feel worse than on the drive down. When they got back to Anna's place, Rena slowly got out of the car. Her stomach wasn't happy and her head was spinning. "Rena!" Anna said as she ran up to grab her as she swayed. "Are you okay?" she asked.

"I'm going to be sick," Rena said. And this time she was.

Rena had never remembered vomiting this much in her life. She felt as it would never end as she leaned into the toilet bowl in Anna's bathroom. Anna held her hair and consoled her friend.

"Oh Rena, I feel terrible," Anna said. "It was probably too much for you in the sun today, and the eel was so rich, I'm so sorry," she wailed tears swimming in her eyes in sympathy for her friend.

Rena looked up at her friend, "Anna, it's okay, I'm really just getting you back for all the times I had to hold your hair in university," she said trying to smile.

Anna laughed for a minute and then looked serious. "I know Rena, I was bad, and you were such a good friend. But this is different. You are not well; we really need to get you to a doctor."

"No, it's okay, I'll be fine," Rena said pushing her friend aside and starting to get up from the floor. She splashed water on her face at the sink and stood up tall. "I feel better now," she said trying to fix a smile on her face." Anna looked at her. "Okay, not great," said Rena diving back down to the bowl where she got sick again.

CHAPTER 25

The next morning Rena woke up to full force nausea. She tried to get out of bed without being sick on the floor and barely made it to the bathroom. She wanted to cry for vomiting again. Anna had stayed with her most of the previous night comforting her and helping her until Rena could not be sick anymore. After a couple of cups of ginger tea, Rena's stomach settled and she went off to bed with promises to let Anna take her to the doctor the next day. She couldn't believe she had been sick again this morning. "I must have a bug," relented Rena to herself. She hated going to the doctor, but she knew Anna was concerned for her, and that she wouldn't be able to hide it. She washed her face and brushed her teeth, and tried to get dressed without feeling sick. "This is brutal," she thought as the peaks of nausea threatened her whenever she moved. How am I going to function? She was about to leave the bedroom when Anna knocked on the door. Rena sat back down on the bed and called Anna in.

"Hey Rena, how are you feeling? Anna said, the look of concern showing on her face.

Rena sighed. "Not great," she said. "I was sick again, and I feel like I might be sick again now," she said unhappily.

"You're going to the doctor then," said Anna sternly.

"I know," said Rena, "I need to go," she sighed.

After a cup of ginger tea that Rena sipped slowly, she started to feel a little better and told Anna she could probably handle the car ride to the doctor in town. They got into the Fiat and Anna drove slowly to the doctor's office. Rena couldn't help but chuckle. "Anna, you are driving like a little old lady!" Rena said giggling.

Anna kept driving looking forward grinning, "I don't want you getting sick on my leather seats Rena," she teased.

"Nice friend you are," said Rena joking, "I mean, what is a little puke between friends?"

Anna giggled and parked on the narrow street in front of the medical centre. Rena got out of the car slowly and followed Anna into the medical centre. She let Anna translate while she waited for an appointment. She wasn't feeling too bad now and wondered if this had all been for nothing. "It will be a waste of money and embarrassing to be here for nothing," she thought. Anna came and sat down beside Rena in the waiting room.

"There's an English speaking doctor here," she said, "so you can go in alone if you want," said Anna.

"Thanks Anna," Rena said, "I'm sure it will be fine. In fact, I'm feeling a lot better now so this might just be for nothing," she said confidently.

The girls sat and read magazines and soon Rena's name was called. She got up from her seat and smiled at her friend as she followed the good-looking doctor into the examination room. Ten minutes later, Rena came back out into the waiting room. Anna jumped up to greet Rena. "That was fast," she said, "What did he say?" she asked anxiously.

"He doesn't think its food poisoning or a bug. He wants me to take a test," Rena said solemnly.

"What kind of test?" Anna asked.

"He thinks I'm *pregnant*!" blurted Rena.

"Holy shit!" Anna said and sat back down.

***

An hour later, Rena after waiting anxiously in the waiting room for the lab to be free, completed the blood test and the girls ventured home. It was unusually quiet in the Fiat on the way back to Anna's home.

"When you do find out for sure?" Anna asked breaking the silence.

"Tomorrow," Rena answered and sighed.

It had been quite a shock when the doctor had suggested she was pregnant. And not expected. Part of her wanted to cry from fear, and another part wanted to cry out for joy. She wasn't sure how to feel, it was confusing.

"How do you think Carl will feel about it Rena?" Anna asked gently as if reading her mind.

"I don't know," Rena said honestly. "It's not

something that ever came up. I know that we had planned to be together back in Toronto, but we definitely did not talk about having a baby. It wasn't something that came up."

She knew Carl loved her. Since he had been back in Bicarri he had called or texted every day, and had always reminded Rena of how he felt about her. She had to admit that she had hoped in the back of her mind that they might get to this step one day, but she hadn't expected anything like this so soon. Anna pulled the Fiat to the side of the road near the shops.

"Wait here," she said. Ten minutes later, she came back into the Fiat and handed Rena a package.

"What is it?" asked Rena.

"Have a look," Anna said grinning.

Rena opened the bag and pulled out a pregnancy test. Anna laughed. "Rena, your face is priceless! Did you really think I could wait until tomorrow?"

When the girls got to Anna's place Rena went to the bathroom to take the test. It was awkward as she had never taken a test before and it took her a minute or two to read and understand the instructions. She came out of the bathroom and almost tripped over Anna who was standing outside the door. "Well," demanded Anna, "Am I going to be an Auntie or what?" she asked.

"It says to wait two minutes," said Rena.

"Bring it to the kitchen," Anna ordered walking away.

"That's gross," said Rena ignoring her and following her to the kitchen. "I'll go and get it in a minute," she said.

In the kitchen, Anna started to get the ingredients ready to bake bread and started warming up soup on the stove. "The soup smells good, I have to admit I'm a bit hungry now," said Rena leaning over the stove to inhale the scent.

"Yah, I figured that, preggos," said Anna kneading the dough for bread.

"Ha-ha, very funny," said Rena taking a banana from the counter and sitting at the table. "I could just have a virus y'know."

"Yah, you *could*, but obviously the doctor thought it was something else," Anna said kneading and punching the dough in front of her.

"Yah," said Rena thoughtfully.

"Go check while I get the bread in the oven," said Anna putting the dough into tins. "And I want to see it, don't throw it away," she called after Rena.

Rena walked into the bathroom. She grabbed the stick from the sink and brought it into the kitchen. She didn't want to look at it. She was scared. A thought had just occurred to her. What if Carl didn't want children? She had never thought of that.

"Oh my god what is it?" Anna said looking at Rena's face when she walked into the kitchen.

"Nothing, I didn't check yet. Anna, I'm scared, what if Carl doesn't want this?" she asked.

"Look Rena, I can tell the guy loves you, and you said it yourself that you guys are going to be going strong in Toronto, so don't worry about it. Any man would be crazy not to want this with you," she said reaching out her hand. "Give me the damn stick," she said, and Rena laughed and handed it to her. Anna took a quick look. "Oh Rena," she said with tears in her eyes. "Congratulations!" She handed the stick to Rena who just stared at it. The realization that she was to become a mother hit her and Rena started to cry. "Rena, don't cry," Anna said putting her arm around her. "It's okay, these things happen all the time, don't worry." You guys love each other right?" Anna reassured her gently. Rena nodded through her tears. "So, it will be okay then, no worries," said Anna consolingly. She went to the counter and came back with a box of tissue. "Now, you wipe your tears, while I get you some food, you are eating for two now," Anna said and turned to check her loaves in the oven.

***

Three hours later after a few hugs and a good cry, Rena was feeling a lot better. Anna had taken control and had pampered her for the rest of the day, ordering her to rest, feeding her when her stomach cooperated and making her ginger tea when it did not. By the time the evening came, Rena felt much like her old self and wanted to go walking with Anna into town for a gelato. They quickly grabbed light sweaters, as the evening was cool, and walked to a local café. The café was large but quiet and they found a table easily, sat down, and ordered the ice creams. Rena ordered a strawberry one and felt like she had never tasted anything so good.

"Oh, I forgot to tell you," Anna exclaimed with a mouthful of chocolate ice cream. Falcone called me when you were resting." Rena's heart jumped. "The guys are going to be coming back in a couple of days and they want to take us to Monte Vergine. I told him I would let him know since you weren't feeling well," she said between spoonfuls.

"Oh, you told him that?" asked Rena beginning to panic.

"Not *that*," said Anna, "just that you were sick, nothing else."

"Ugh Anna," lamented Rena. "I didn't tell Carl that I wasn't feeling great. Not sure why, but I didn't want him to worry. Now he will be texting me all night I bet," she said.

"Well you have to tell him sometime," said Anna insistently.

"Yah, but not yet," said Rena, "and definitely not by text."

"I'm sorry Rena, I should have kept my mouth shut," Anna said sorrowfully.

"No worries, I am just being sensitive, it's okay," Rena responded smiling at her friend.

They finished their ice creams and then walked quietly around the town park enjoying the cooler air. "I just don't know what I am going to do," said Rena breaking the silence.

"Well, don't worry about it yet," said Anna. "Talk to Carl, I am sure it will all work out," she said smiling touching Rena's arm.

"True," said Rena relaxing. After all, he *loved* her. *What could go wrong?*

CHAPTER 26

The next day Rena received the results of the test as she was finishing her breakfast. Her heart was beating a mile a minute as she answered the call and Anna put her arm around her friend for support. The nurse on the line told Rena that she was definitely pregnant but early enough that she had to be careful, get lots of rest and ensure she had proper nutrition. Rena hung up the phone, and turned to Anna and gave her a big hug. Her talks with Anna the other day had helped and Rena felt more positive about the new experience she was going through, although she could really give up the nausea. She had taken another turn of nausea that morning and had spent half an hour in the bathroom. But, after that, she had started to feel better and had even got down some bread and tea. Carl and Falcone were due back in the evening and Rena was excited. She was not sure she was ready to tell Carl yet, but she had missed him and was ready to see him again. True to form he had texted her many times the previous evening when he had found out from Falcone she wasn't feeling well. But Rena had assured him she was fine, even when he called to make sure. Anna had looked at her somewhat disapprovingly. Rena knew Anna wanted her to come clean with Carl, but Rena wasn't ready for that yet. It was early days. *There was time.*

They went to church midday with Zio Augusto and Teresa. Neither girl had really wanted to go, but Anna felt that she had to spend time with her aunt and uncle since she had been away. Rena was a little worried her stomach would act up, but thankfully it was okay and she got to the mass in one piece. The mass was in Italian so Rena looked around, and did some people watching. She giggled a little when she noticed a woman in the pew giving the priest a sign that his sermon was too long. The woman sighed loudly and used a fan to cool herself off to show her annoyance as she glanced at the heavens in despair. Rena nudged Anna and both girls stifled a laugh. After the service, Anna made excuses to her aunt and uncle and the girls returned home to have a quiet meal of steamed rice and grilled vegetables.

The rest of the afternoon Rena and Anna sunbathed in the backyard, read books and relaxed. Anna went into the house, came back out, and shoved a book into Rena's hands. "What to Expect When You're Expecting." The realization hit Rena like a ton of bricks. "Oh my god, Anna, I'm so sorry, I forgot. How selfish of me," Rena said.

"It's okay Rena, it was a long time ago," Anna said softly. "I want this to be a good experience for you," she said rubbing Rena's arm.

"Yes, but here I was talking about feeling weird about being pregnant, and you were, and you lost your baby. I'm so sorry Anna, I can't believe I forgot, I am such a cow," Rena lamented.

Anna laughed. "No, you are not a cow, yet, but you will be. Nice and fat with huge ankles!" Anna said teasing.

"Really, I am sorry Anna. How thoughtless of me," Rena said standing up to hug her friend. "I don't deserve you Anna, you are so good to me," Rena said.

"That is rubbish," said Anna holding Rena at arm's length. "Seriously, don't let me ever hear you say that again," she said vehemently. "You deserve the best Rena, YOU! Don't forget that; don't let a bad marriage pull you down. You deserved better then, and you deserve better now. You deserve all that is good. And if that good is having a wonderful friend like me, then it is," she said pulling Rena close and hugging her. "I love you Rena," Anna said.

"I love you too Anna," Rena said, tears in her eyes.

CHAPTER 27

Rena woke up early. The guys hadn't made it the night before due to a work issue that came up but had promised to be there in the morning to take the girls to Monte Vergine. Rena stumbled to the bathroom. It hadn't been long but she was starting to get used to the morning nausea if that was possible. After sitting on the bathroom floor for ten minutes, Rena felt like she had enough strength to get up. She was excited and pensive to see Carl today. She had talked to him last night on the phone and he had sounded down that he could not see her. She could hear the concern in his voice that she had been sick and she felt bad pretending it was just a flu. She didn't want him to find out on the phone. She wanted to tell him when the time was right; she wanted it to be special. She could feel the excitement rise up in her thinking of the child that was growing insider her. It was hers and Carl's. The thought that their love had brought about this made her heart soar. She had never thought that she could find a love like this, a man like this, let alone have a child with him. She couldn't wait to tell him. At the back of her mind though, something was making her worry. She wasn't sure why and figured it was just hormones and quickly brushed it off.

***

They arrived in Ariano Irpino at 8 am. Carl had been anxious to get on the road to see Rena and had practically pulled Falcone out of bed by the feet to get him going. It had only been a week but Carl had missed Rena. He missed her smile, her kisses, that body. He could feel himself getting aroused just thinking of her. *What she did to him.* He couldn't wait to hold her in his arms again all night. He wasn't sure if Rena had cleared it with Anna but he was planning to spend the night with her come hell or high water. His next stretch in Bicarri would run almost three weeks with only a couple days in between so he needed all the Rena time he could get. Plus, he felt she wasn't telling him something. That she was sicker than she let on. When he had talked to her last night, her voice had sounded funny, almost insecure. He needed to know why. He didn't want her to feel insecure when it came to him. He was going nowhere.

Falcone drove up to Anna's house and both men got out of the car. Rena came out to greet them and Carl rushed over to her and pulled her close to him. "God I missed you Rena," he said planting a kiss on her neck and then moving to her mouth.

"I missed you too," smiled Rena kissing him back and looking into his eyes.

He stared at her. Her eyes looked tired but something about her was different. He couldn't put his finger on it. "Are you feeling okay?" he asked Rena stroking her hair and putting it behind her ear.

"Yes, I feel better, it was just a virus or too much sun," she said looking down and playing with the lapel on his shirt.

"Are you sure?" Carl asked trying to get Rena to look back up at him.

"Yes," she said looking up and then grabbing his arm and pulling him into the house.

"Everything okay?" he asked pulling her back.

"Yes, of course," Rena said. "Let's go have something to eat before we go," she said smiling.

But her eyes did not smile as usual. Something was up. He knew it.

***

They had a great breakfast of eggs, fresh bread, cheese, jam and coffee and then cleaned up quickly so they could get on the road. Rena had passed on the coffee raving about the ginger tea that Anna had found at the store. She could see Carl looking at her oddly. She knew he knew something was up but she hoped he wouldn't figure it out before she told him.

They all climbed into Falcone's fiat and drove the route from Ariano Irpino to Monte Vergine. They passed Grottaminarda on the way and Falcone commented to Carl and Rena that they had the best pizza in the area. "Oh, we went there already," said Anna.

"Really?" said Falcone. "Rena, great pizza don't you think?" he asked.

"Yes, it was great," Rena said trying not to remember how her evening with Anna had ended a couple nights before.

"What did you guys have?" Falcone asked.

Anna started describing the pizza and Rena could feel her stomach recall the events of the other day. The thought of that pizza or any pizza right now made her feel sick. She had tried to stick to bread during breakfast but she didn't want Carl to notice anything besides the tea so she had eaten an egg. But now it wasn't sitting right. She sat in the back of Fiat trying to look straight so her stomach wouldn't churn. The roads were curvy winding up to the mount and Rena could feel herself beginning to sweat. Carl opened the window to let in the cooler mountain air. Rena took a deep breath.

"Rena, are you okay," Anna whispered to her in the back seat.

"Feeling a bit sick, but the air is helping," whispered Rena.

"Are you going to tell him today?" Anna whispered.

"I guess so," said Rena noticing Carl cocking his head to hear them.

"What are you girls chatting about back there?" he asked.

"Nothing you want to know about," said Anna boldly. "Unless you want to know all about the period I am having. It really is brutal," she said with a smirk.

"Okay enough," Carl interrupted and Falcone grunted in agreement. "We don't need to know."

Rena started to relax with the cool breeze from outside the car caressing her face, and began to notice how beautiful the drive up to Monte Vergine was. Falcone started to explain to her and Carl that the mountain was

160

1270 feet above sea level and that people from all over Italy go there and visit the monastery as it is said to be a place of miracles. "There is also a legend that if you are a virgin and have sex on the hill, you leave the mountain still a virgin," he said. "Guess it's too late for either of you in the back to test that one out," he said laughing.

Anna smacked him on the back of the head and let off a hurl of Italian expletives. "I don't know what you said Anna, but that sounded lovely," Rena said laughing.

They got to the car park and walked with the crowds to the church of the monastery. Carl grabbed Rena's hand and gave her a small smile. *He's still worried about me*, she thought. They followed Anna and Falcone into the church and Rena gasped. She had never seen such a sight. The ceilings and walls were adorned with paintings, made of gold and marble of different colours. It was so beautiful that Rena shivered. Carl took her into his arms and held her close. "I'm so glad that I got to see this with you Rena, it's phenomenal," he said.

"Me too," said Rena holding him close.

They walked further into the church, took seats in a pew, and looked around. Rena was happy to sit, as her stomach was still not on level ground. Carl sat beside her and put his arm around her. "It's great to see this, but I am so glad I got to see you again," he said.

"Yes, me too, I missed you Carl," Rena said.

"Rena, are you sure you are feeling okay?" asked Carl, "You seem a bit quieter than usual," he said sounding concerned.

"Yes, but Carl, I have to tell you something," Rena said turning in the pew to look at him. This was a beautiful place, and a place of miracles, it was a perfect place to tell him. "Carl, I…"

"Hey guys, let's go back outside and walk around," interrupted Anna popping her head in between them from the pew behind.

"Ah," Rena looked at Carl with a half-smile and a shrug. "Okay let's go," she said smiling at Anna and getting up.

They walked outside the monastery enjoying the cool air and the spectacular views of the countryside below. Anna and Rena left the guys outside and dipped into the gift shop to look at the souvenirs and religious articles for sale. "Anna, you really have bad timing," Rena said to her friend. "I was about to tell him."

"Oh seriously?" asked Anna. "Rena, I'm sorry. Do you want me to get Falcone so we can leave you guys alone to talk?"

"No, don't worry about it now," said Rena, "I will find the right time," she said reassuringly. The girls went back outside to greet Falcone and Carl who were ready to head back.

"I promised my parents we would have lunch with them," said Falcone. "Plus, since I won't be bringing any virgins back down the mountain, we might as well leave," he said teasing.

Anna tried to slap Falcone again but he ducked, right into Rena who gave him a playful slap on the wrist. "You're terrible," joked Rena.

"I could respond to that, but Carl would kill me," said Falcone mischievously.

"Find your own virgin," Carl growled grabbing Rena's arm. They all laughed and kept it up as they went back to the car.

The ride back was scenic and eventful with Falcone continuing his teasing and the rest of them chiming in to put him down when they could. It was light and fun and Rena could feel her body settling into normalcy. They arrived at Zio Augusto and Zia Teresa's and sat down to a lunch of pasta, peas, chicken, and watermelon and pears for dessert. They chatted amicably with stories of Falcone and Anna as kids and all the escapades and trouble they got into. They all burst into laughter a few times, as Zio Augusto recounted stories of getting Falcone's head out of a fence and Anna getting her hair stuck in the pasta maker. Rena looked at Carl. He smiled at her and looked at her intently. *I have to tell him tonight*, she thought. It can't wait.

CHAPTER 28

They spent most of the afternoon and evening at
Falcone's house and it wasn't until 7 pm that they decided
to go back to Anna's place. Rena felt tired. She knew it
must be all of the changes her body was going through,
and she was exhausted. She was going to have to ask
Anna for a cappuccino so she could stay awake. She hoped
that she could stomach it. They arrived back at the house
and decided to have a drink in the backyard. It was a nice
summer evening and the kind of weather to sit out.
Falcone grabbed a bottle of red wine from Anna's wine
rack and started searching in her kitchen for an opener.
"Anna, where is the opener?" he asked opening drawer
after drawer.

"Calm down, Falc, it's right here," Anna said picking up
an opener from on top of the wine rack and grabbing the
bottle from Falcone.

Falcone reached up and got four glasses from the
cupboard. "Actually Falcone, I'm going to have
something else," said Rena glancing at Anna and hoping
she would catch on.

"Really?" Carl piped in, "I thought you loved red wine," he said.

"I do, actually, but I'm not really in the mood. A cappuccino would go down very nicely though," said Rena looking at Anna.

"Oh," said Anna, "Are you sure?"

"Holy cow," thought Rena, "Did she forget already?" "Yah sure," she said trying to give Anna a long stare.

"Okay," Anna said shrugging her shoulders and leaning down to get out the espresso maker.

Anna made the cappuccino and the four of them moved to the backyard with their drinks. Rena sipped the cappuccino slowly. She wasn't sure how her stomach would react but the warm milky drink went down well. Carl looked over at Rena's mug. "That looks more like a latte than a cappuccino," he said giving Rena a kiss on the cheek.

Anna giggled. "I made a mistake," she said, "I guess it is a latte. Is it okay Rena?" she asked.

Rena could have sworn Anna winked at her but wasn't sure. "Yes, it's great," said Rena, "Creamy and smooth, I love it," she said.

They spent a few hours in the backyard talking and enjoying the weather and music that Anna played from her outdoor speakers. It was comfortable and cozy and Rena felt at peace. She could imagine sitting here with Carl and their baby running around in the garden while they talked. The thought made her smile and she knew that she had to let Carl know soon.

***

Rena yawned. "God she is beautiful when she yawns," thought Carl. He could tell that she wasn't over whatever illness she had had. The summer night was warm and breezy and he could see the tendrils of her hair touch her face. It drove him wild and he wanted to play with them, amongst other things, the whole night long. But he could tell something wasn't right, that she still wasn't feeling well. It would disappoint him to not be able to make love to her tonight, but holding her all night would be okay. As long as he could be there when she awoke in the morning. It was important to him that he be there. He knew her husband had disappointed her, that she had felt unloved and undeserving. That she had loved him. He wanted desperately to show her how love could be. How it was when it was reciprocated the way it should be. He didn't know if Jarod had loved her or not. It wasn't for him to say. Some people didn't know how to show love, or be loving, but he knew from experience that they still felt it. He could only try to give Rena what he knew she had missed. And he wanted to give it to her. He *had* to give it to her. It was important to him.

Rena yawned again, and Carl tousled her hair. "Com'on sleepy head, let's take you to bed," he said. Rena let out a small sigh and gave him such a disarming smile that he almost ignored his intuition to let her rest, and instead pick her up and take her to bed to show her how many parts he had missed kissing the many nights before. But he couldn't. She did look tired, and he wanted her to be well. He smiled at her and took her hand. "Let's go," he said. Rena ambled up and Carl put his arm around her waist. "Let me tuck you in, sweetheart," he said.

She had forced him to look at her. "You never look at me," she had said. "Yes I do," he said, but he was still playing a game on his phone. She stared at him. "You are still playing on the phone," she said, "Is it more important than me?" "No," he had said, "But I need to finish this game." "Soul mates look into each other's eyes a lot," she said. He continued playing and then sighed and put the phone down and looked at her. She looked into his eyes. "You never talk to me," she said, "I never know what is going on." "I am an open book," he said. "But your idea of open hurts," she thought. She looked into his eyes again. They were different eyes, brown eyes; the most deep brown she had ever seen. They were gentle, kind, swimming with love. "I love you," the voice with the eyes said. "I love you and will love you forever."

***

Rena woke up, her stomach doing somersaults. She could feel Carl's body next to hers and his arms around her. It would have been wonderful had she not had this morning nausea. But his arms around her waist made her feel even sicker. She remembered him tucking her in the night before. He had been so loving, so kind. She had wanted him to make love to her, but her eyes would not stay open, and he had gently kissed them closed and told her to rest. She had felt him get into the bed next to her and take her in his arms. She didn't remember much after that. She knew he had stayed in the bed with her the whole night. She turned her head. She could feel his breath rise and fall next to her and she knew he was still sleeping. She had to get downstairs quickly. Her stomach was acting up, and if the last few days had been any indication, she knew that she didn't have much time to spare before the contents were cleared out.

She slowly moved away from him in the bed and carefully moved his arms off her body and back onto the bed. She slipped on her robe and turned back to look at him. She loved him. She loved this man. She turned and tiptoed out of the room and silently closed the door. She could feel her stomach begin to wretch and she quickly ran down the stairs into the bathroom near the kitchen. She just made it before she vomited everything out into the toilet. She sighed and then sat on the ground, grabbing the

167

hand towel to wipe her face.

"What the hell?"

Rena turned. Falcone stood at the doorway to the bathroom. "Rena, are you still sick?" he asked sounding concerned.

Before Rena could answer she turned and wretched into the toilet again. "No," she said, "I mean, ugh," she said as she vomited again.

"Holy shit, Rena are you sure you're okay?" he asked moving closer to grab her another towel.

"Yes, I'm fine but I need to tell Carl," she said panting, exhausted from the sickness.

"Tell me what?" Rena turned and looked up at Carl his body framed in the doorway.

"I didn't want to tell you this way," Rena said the tears welling in her eyes.

Carl quickly went into the bathroom and dropped down to her side. "Rena, please tell me, what is wrong, are you okay?" he asked framing her face with his hands.

"I-I'm pregnant," Rena said the tears starting to well out of her eyes.

"How, could you be," Falcone started.

"It's true," Rena said looking at Carl.

"Pregnant?" She could see him mouth the words but his voice didn't sound right. "Pregnant, Rena, you are *pregnant?*" Carl said in disbelief.

He didn't look right. His face was a mix of emotion she

couldn't understand. "Yes, sorry, I, meant to tell you last night, but I was so tired," she said, smiling at him and wiping her face again with the towel.

"Really," said Carl staring at her like he didn't know her.

Rena shook her head. He sounded sarcastic, almost angry. She couldn't be right; she must be delirious. "I forgot to tell you, I meant to. But it's a good thing, we love each other," she said trying to smile up at him again.

"Holy shit Rena!" Falcone interrupted sounding annoyed.

What was going on? Something wasn't right. She wasn't sure if it was her stomach, or her mind, but something was wrong. Neither Carl nor Falcone seemed very happy with her. "I-I'm pregnant," she told the guys looking at Carl.

"*How,*" demanded Falcone.

"How?" squeaked Rena. How? She looked at Carl. His eyes looked cold and distant and something in Rena's heart died. In that instant, she felt scared. Something was wrong. "What's wrong?" she asked looking at Carl. His face looked pale.

"He can't have kids, Rena," Falcone shouted, pointing at Carl and looking at her as if she was crazy. "He can't have kids," he repeated flailing his arms and walking away.

Rena looked at Carl. What was going on? What was Falcone talking about? She looked back at Carl. He was looking at her like was a stranger. Something welled up inside her and she felt horrified. "B-but, that's impossible," she said. She could feel the room swim around her, and then it went black.

CHAPTER 29

She came to on the couch. She could hear people above her talking but she couldn't make out what they were saying. She could hear Carl, he sounded upset, worried. It took her a couple of minutes to realize where she was and then all of the memories of the bathroom came back. What had happened? She tried to sit up. She had to know what was going on.

"Rena," Anna looked at her from above the couch. "Are you okay honey?" she said moving to the other side of the couch to kneel by Rena.

"W-Where's Carl?" Rena said trying to sit up.

"He's with Falcone, Rena, we have to talk," Anna said gently pushing Rena back down on the couch.

"No, I have to talk to him, I don't know what is going on," Rena pleaded feeling the anxiety well up in her chest.

"Rena," Anna said, "Listen to me."

"I can't, I need to see him," Rena said trying again to get

up. The room started spinning again and she lay back down.

"Rena, take it easy, calm down," Anna said gently pausing until Rena relaxed against the couch pillow.

"What's going on?" Rena asked looking at her friend.

"Rena," Anna paused, "Did you know that Carl couldn't have children?" Anna asked.

What? Rena's eyes swam, she felt sick. "I'm going to be sick," she said getting up and stumbling to the bathroom. The room was spinning and Rena barely made it to the bathroom before she vomited. Anna followed her and held her hair back as she got sick. She grabbed a wet cloth from the sink and gave it to Rena who wiped her mouth and face.

"I don't get it," said Rena. "How is this possible? "He never told me he couldn't have children, but obviously it isn't true, since I am *pregnant*!" she said starting to get frustrated. "Is this his way to get out of it?" she asked nobody in particular.

"Rena, did you guys never talk about this?" Anna asked sounding shocked.

"No!" Rena cried. "He never told me. You would think that would have come up."

"Yah you would think," muttered Anna under the breath.

"But either way," Rena continued, "It doesn't make sense since I am *pregnant*!" She couldn't believe what was happening. Did he not want children so much as to deny that one could exist? She didn't understand how this could be happening or what was going on.

"Rena," Anna said gently sitting beside her on the bathroom floor. "You know I love you, and that I would never judge you, but did you meet anyone else here in town? Maybe someone that you had a fling with?" Anna asked gently.

Rena was floored. The world that she knew was turned upside down. Her best friend. Even her best friend did not believe her. All of her dreams felt instantly shattered. She had to talk to Carl. She had to find out what was going on. None of it made sense. "I need to talk to Carl," she said getting up off the floor.

"Rena, I didn't mean to offend you," Anna said. "But if what they say is true, how can you be pregnant with Carl's baby?" she asked following her out of the bathroom. "I know he had cancer Rena, so maybe he can't have children, I don't know," she said looking at Rena dejectedly.

Rena stared back at her friend. She didn't even recognize her. Who was this person? The Anna she knew would stick by her and defend her. This Anna seemed just as confused as Rena was.

"Where is Carl?" Rena demanded looking around for the guys.

"They went for a drive for a bit, they'll be back," Anna said. "Come to the kitchen and I will make you a tea and something to eat. You still need to take care of your baby," she said looking at Rena earnestly.

Rena followed Anna into the kitchen. Right now she didn't want anything, but to maybe punch Anna. She was still in her robe and held it tightly around her. Somehow, it felt comforting to have something wrapped around her.

The kitchen was silent. Even Anna, who normally had a lot to say, was quiet. Rena was glad. If Anna said anymore, she wasn't sure their friendship could be saved. She was furious at her friend and felt betrayed. She took the tea that Anna offered and tried to eat some bread but it tasted like sawdust and stuck in her mouth. She needed to see Carl. She needed him to know that this was his baby. To hell with what anybody else thought. *He was the father.*

***

When she fainted, Carl felt like his world had fallen apart. He reached over, caught her, and lay her gently on the coach. His head was spinning. He needed her to be okay. But his heart was in turmoil. He hadn't told her he couldn't have kids. He knew he should have, but somehow it had gotten away from him. And now, *this*. He wasn't sure how she could be pregnant. It wasn't his; he knew that. But what had happened? He had to know. Maybe it was before he met her, but it couldn't have been. He remembered that first night with her, and how she had tensed up when he entered her. There was no way that she had been with someone just before him. He sighed. It didn't make sense. He could see Anna hovering over her and could see that she was waking up. He breathed a sigh of relief that she was okay, but the breath got stuck in his chest and he couldn't let it go. He felt like the wind had been knocked out of him and stood back, trying to catch his breath.

"Hey buddy," Falcone said. "Breathe, Carl, com'on man, breathe, let it out," Falcone said from beside him.

He needed air. "Air" he choked out stumbling out of the house.

Falcone followed him to the laneway. "Get in the car buddy, let's just get away from here for a bit," Falcone said.

Carl stumbled into the car. Falcone got in the driver seat and started driving through the town. Carl looked out the window his chest bursting with pain as he tried to breathe. They drove past the park where they had danced, past the church where they had kissed; she was everywhere. Falcone drove out of town and stopped at a rural spot at the side of the road. Carl jumped out of the car and moved quickly into the field. He fell to his knees. The pain in his chest was excruciating. Falcone came behind him and put a hand on his shoulder. "Breathe, let it out," he said.

Carl breathed deeply and released the breath that had a hold of his chest. The pain intensified and then subsided. He breathed again and could feel the pain in his heart. This pain wasn't physical; it was worse. He breathed in again and looked up at the sky. And then he looked down and breathed out, and wept.

CHAPTER 30

She knew he was there before she saw him. She *felt* him. She turned as he walked into the kitchen with Falcone. Rena looked up at him and was shocked. His eyes were red and he looked pale. "Carl," she said getting up.

Carl looked into her eyes. Rena could see the pain that he couldn't shield. She moved forward but Falcone stopped her.

"Let's just all sit down and talk," said Falcone moving her back.

"I need to talk to Carl alone," said Rena gaining some strength giving Falcone a push aside. She needed answers and she needed them from Carl.

"Yes, Falcone, Rena and I need to talk alone," Carl answered looking right at Rena. His voice sounded shaky and at that instant Rena's heart shattered into a thousand pieces.

"Okay Falcone," Anna said looking at Rena, "Let's take our coffee outside." "Let's go," she said sternly when

Falcone didn't move. She poured three cups of coffee and gestured to Falcone to get the two mugs while she added a third on to the table for Carl. "Here Carl, sit down," she said.

"Let me know if you need me buddy," Falcone said walking outside.

Rena glared at Falcone's back. She wasn't sure why, but in an instant Falcone's loyalty had been lost with her.

Carl moved over from his side of the table to sit beside Rena. He took her hands and looked deeply into her eyes. "Rena," he said, lifting her hands and kissing them slowly. He looked up and Rena could see tears swimming his eyes.

"Carl," said she moving one of her hands to stroke his cheek. "Don't cry, please don't cry," Rena said feeling her own tears drip slowly down her face.

"Rena," Carl said wiping the tears from his eyes. "Please be honest with me. I love you, you can tell me anything," he said. He looked at her waiting.

Rena looked at him. "I-it's your baby," she said bursting into tears. "I don't know why you don't b-believe me," she cried.

Carl sighed. "Rena, I can't have children," he said. "Believe me, if I could I would. There is no way this child can be mine," he said.

"How do you know?" Rena cried. "How do you know? You're the only one I have been with. Maybe things have changed, maybe you can have children now," she cried.

"Ugh," Carl said sighing again and sounded frustrated and he put his head in his hands. He lifted his head up and looked directly at Rena. "Rena, do you love me?" he asked looking at her searchingly.

"Of course I do, you know I do!" Rena said through her tears.

Carl nodded. "Then, tell me the truth," he said.

Rena felt floored. He didn't believe her. "I *am* telling you the truth!" she cried standing up from the chair knocking it down. "I haven't had anything with anybody but you in Italy, or even in Toronto. Nobody!" she cried angrily.

"Rena!" Carl responded sounding angry, "I have been through this before, I got tested a few years ago, and there is no way this baby could be mine. Just talk to me, BE HONEST Rena," he pleaded still sounding annoyed.

"*Be honest? Be honest?*" Rena could hear her voice rising shrilly through her tears. "Nice for you to say," she cried angrily. "You didn't tell me you couldn't have children. I would think that should have come up at some point, um, geeze, *maybe* between, I love you and I want to be with you in Toronto?" she cried kicking the chair in front of her.

"Rena, sit down," Carl said.

"No," said Rena defiantly. "You don't believe me. You love me but you don't believe me, what a joke!" Rena cried trying to move past Carl.

Carl stood up and grabbed Rena's arm. "Rena, I do love you," he said sounding annoyed. "You know I do."

"Give me a break," Rena cried.

"I know Rena, I should have told you I couldn't have children, I admit that. But it doesn't change the fact that I can't, and this child cannot be mine," he said looking at her sternly.

Rena stared at him. This man. The man she loved and had poured her heart out to. The man she had let the barriers down for. The only person she had trusted to not judge her about her marriage to Jarod. The man who had made her feel loved and loveable again. The man who was now dismissing her words. The man who denied what she was saying. The man who did not believe her. At this moment, she realized that hated him. "Just get out," she said slowly and quietly backing up in the kitchen.

Carl walked toward her, "Rena, we need to talk, we have to talk about this," Carl said.

"Get out!" Rena screamed. Carl's face turned white. "Get out, I hate you, get out!" she screamed. She could see his eyes fill with tears.

"Okay," he said quietly holding up his hands. He turned to walk out the backdoor and paused. Rena could hear him sigh. And then he left.

**

She didn't come out of the bedroom for hours. She had heard Anna knock on the door a few times earlier in the day, and now she heard her again. "Just go away," Rena called out rolling onto the other side on the bed.

"Rena, please, let me in," pleaded Anna. "Please, if only for the baby. You need to calm down, and get something to eat."

Rena sighed. She knew Anna was right. But she couldn't move. She kept replaying the events in her head. And his face, the look on his face. She couldn't get that out of her head. She felt the tears drip down her cheeks. How was she ever going to get over this?

"Rena, please." She could hear Anna again.

"Go fuck yourself," Rena thought ignoring her.

***

Rena woke up. She had cried herself to sleep from all the stress in the morning. She heard Anna's footsteps outside the door. "Rena?" she could hear Anna tentatively call through the door.

She sounded upset, like she had been crying. Rena sat up in the bed her heart aching for her friend. "I might as well let her in," Rena thought, "Anna isn't giving up." "Come in," she called out. Anna came in with a tear stained face, took one look at Rena, and ran to hug her.

"Oh Rena," she said hugging her friend in her arms. "Oh Rena, I am so sorry," she wailed hanging on to Rena, "I am a horrible friend," she cried.

Rena's resolve broke. She clung to her friend. "Oh Anna, how could this have happened?" Rena sobbed.

"I don't know honey, I don't know," said Anna stroking her back and rocking her gently. "This is all so confusing," Anna said.

Rena held tightly onto her friend and sobbed. "I-I thought he loved me," she cried. Anna pulled Rena away to look at her.

"Rena, he *does* love you that I know," she said through her tears.

"But he left?" Rena cried.

"Rena you told him to leave," Anna said. "But he still wants to talk to you."

"About what?" Rena cried, "He doesn't believe the baby is his, so what is there to talk about?" Rena started sobbing again. She felt as if her heart could break no more. It was shattered, pulverized, a mound of dust.

"I think you should talk to him Rena," Anna said gently wiping her tears. "Just hear him out," she said.

Rena took in a deep breath. She had wanted to hear him out, but he had not *heard her*. He had not believed that this child could be is. He had assumed it wasn't right away. "And maybe he had a point," she thought, "Because he couldn't have kids, but things happen, they could happen couldn't they?" Rena took another deep breath.

"Rena, I am so sorry," Anna said looking at her.

"I know," Rena said.

"Come down for some food, okay? For the baby?" Anna asked.

"Yes, I will," said Rena, "I'll be down in a minute. I am just going to wash up first."

Anna left the room and Rena slowly got up, went to the bathroom, and splashed water on her face. The cool water felt good on her tear stained skin. She patted her face dry and walked out of the bathroom noticing the flashing on her phone. She had turned it off when she had asked him to leave. She had needed space and time to think. She looked at the phone and noticed a message from Carl. She tapped the phone. It was one line. *I love you*, it said. Rena stared at the phone. She tapped to reply; then threw the phone on the bed and walked downstairs.

Anna was in the kitchen when she got here stirring soup on the stove. She turned around when she heard Rena. "Hey, you look a little better," she said with an unsure smile.

Rena wanly smiled back. "I'm okay," she said sighing. I'm okay."

"Rena, I'm sorry what I said earlier, I didn't want to hurt you but..."

"I don't want to talk about this Anna," Rena interrupted. "Let's just eat and relax. Please," she said.

Anna nodded, "Of course," she said turning back to the stove.

Anna dished out the soup and got a loaf of fresh bread out of the oven. She brought it to the table and Rena ate hungrily. "This baby is going to make me fat," she said, "That was soo good."

Anna smiled. "This is what we feed all the pregnant mothers," she said, "so that they stay fat forever," she said wickedly looking at Rena.

Rena laughed and touched Anna's arm. It felt good to laugh. She loved Anna; she could always make her smile, even when she was mad at her. "Well," she said, "since that is the plan, I will have some more," and got up to help herself to more soup from the stove.

They spent a quiet evening chatting and neither of them brought up the events of the day. Falcone called twice in the evening and Rena could hear Anna chatting excitedly with him on the phone in Italian. She wasn't sure what was being said, but from what she could tell from Anna's face and gestures, Falcone was getting a good stripping down. Rena snuggled into the couch. She was glad that Anna was sticking up for her.

Anna came back into the living room. "That was Falcone

181

again," she said sitting down with a big sigh.

Rena looked at her friend. "What did he want?" she asked innocently.

"He wants you to talk to Carl," she said. "I told him you weren't ready, and then he said he was going to come over here. I told him I would kill him first," she said vehemently shaking her fist in the air.

Rena laughed. "Are you serious?"

"Yes," said Anna looking surprised. "Wait- Wasn't I supposed to do that?" she asked anxiously.

"Yes," said Rena moving over to where Anna sat to give her friend a big hug. "Thanks Anna." She smiled at her friend.

"You know I am always here for you, don't you Rena?" Anna asked anxiously.

"I know Anna, I know," she said smiling. And she believed it.

CHAPTER 31

Rena woke up the next morning feeling exhausted. The previous day's events had been tiring emotionally and physically and she didn't feel like getting up. She knew Anna was going to the market this morning and had errands to run, but she didn't feel like joining her. It had taken awhile for Rena to fall asleep the night before, and after crying for a couple of hours, it had become clear to her what she had to do. She lay in the bed praying for the strength to get up and follow through on her decision. This was probably one of the hardest things she ever had to do. Her eyes welled with tears. "No, no more crying," she said to herself, wiping the one that escaped.

She heard Anna's Fiat leave the drive and she forced herself up. Her stomach did a double take and she did a mad dash to the bathroom. She got to the toilet in time and quickly vomited, and then got up slowly to wash her face. She stared into the mirror. She looked different. Sure, her eyes were puffy from the crying, but she looked different. "I guess what they say is true about pregnant woman," she said looking into the mirror. "We look different."

Rena picked up a toothbrush and tried to brush her teeth without feeling the need to vomit. After successfully brushing her teeth and swishing some mouthwash around her mouth, she walked out of the bathroom. She made her way to the dresser, picked out a pair of shorts and a t-shirt and quickly got dressed. She sat on the bed and looked around. She had had great times in Italy. It had been wonderful, life changing, happy and desperately sad all at the same time. She sighed and then slowly got her suitcase out of the closet. One by one, she took her clothes out of the closet, folded them and put them into the suitcase.

Half an hour later she was done. She stood at the door to the bedroom and glanced back around the room where she had spent the last while. Where she had found love and lost love. She turned away slowly and walked down the stairs. In the kitchen, she quickly got some bread with jam and made a cup of tea. When she was done, she washed her dishes and wrote a quick note to Anna, explaining her decision and asking for forgiveness for not saying goodbye. She felt bad leaving this way, but she felt that she had no choice. Carl had been pretty clear. "I need to get away and start a life with my baby," she thought. Rena left the note on the kitchen table and rolled her suitcase to the front door. She had seen the bus routes in town and she knew she could catch a bus to Naples and get a flight from there. She closed the door to Anna's place and sighed. "God bless you Anna," she said to herself and slowly walked down the driveway.

***

Carl woke up with a tremendous hangover. His head was banging and felt like it weighed a hundred pounds. He couldn't move it without it feeling the room begin to spin. His mouth felt like sawdust and his body ached all over. He admonished himself for drinking so much the night before. He couldn't handle what was happening. And, the worse part was, he felt that somehow a lot of it was his own fault. *He should have told her.* He should have been open with her. But he was scared. She was so beautiful and so loving that she tore the shutters he had on his heart and had taken a hold of it. And he liked it. He loved it. He loved it so much that he hadn't been honest with her. Too afraid to lose what he was loving so much. But he realized now that it was selfish and that his worse fears had come true. He had lost her even when he had tried to hold on to her so tightly. He sighed and tried to get up off the couch. His head pounded and his stomach did somersaults. This was his punishment. He couldn't believe it when she had told him to get out. She had sounded hurt and angry. But the look he saw in her eyes had hurt the most. She had looked like she *hated* him.

He could hear Falcone and Zia Teresa in the kitchen. It had taken a huge effort to get off the bed, and Carl was surprised that he had made it down the stairs in one piece. He stumbled into the kitchen and grumbled a quick "Bounjourno," and sat down at the table. Zia Teresa quickly brought him an espresso and Carl drained it quickly. She made a few remarks in Italian that he couldn't comprehend and went to the stove to get him another one. Falcone put a glass of water in front of him.

"Here you go buddy, you probably need this more than espresso," he said turning to look at his mother. "Ma, he needs water, not coffee."

Zia Teresa answered Falcone in another spatter of Italian. Carl could hardly make out the words his head hurt so much, but he knew she wasn't happy. "No, its okay," he said in English trying desperately to search for the Italian words that would not come. Zia Teresa put the espresso in front of him with a biscotti and Carl dipped the cookie into the hot liquid. He bit the cookie. His stomach seemed to agree with the mixture and Carl

185

continued to dip and taste it, not looking up from his cup.

"Buddy," Falcone said beside him. "You really should go and try and talk to her today."

Carl sighed. Falcone was right, that much he knew. But he wasn't sure how to approach her. They were both hurt and angry, and he didn't want a repeat of the night before. He wanted her to know that he loved her, and that he was sorry for not telling her that he could not have children. He wanted to tell her that they could move through anything, even a mistake. But he needed her to be open. She had been so insistent that the child was his that it scared him. All kinds of things went through his mind last night and he wondered if something had happened to her in Italy that she was not aware of. The thought of this made his stomach churn again. *I have to see her.* Even if she would not talk, he had to make her listen. He finished the espresso and got up from the kitchen table thanking Zia Teresa for the food and giving her a small hug. She still seemed annoyed with him but gave him a pat on the back. "At least that is something," he thought. Carl turned to look at Falcone. "Care to drive me to Anna's?" he asked.

"I'll drive you buddy, but seriously you have to take a shower first, you smell like the bar," Falcone said with a huge grin.

"Good point," said Carl. She probably didn't want to see him, but at least he could try to look his best.

CHAPTER 32

Rena walked into town pulling her suitcase behind her. She had seen the bus stop in town, and knew she could take it to where she was going. She arrived at the bus station and bought a ticket; then sat on a bench and waited around. She felt tired. She knew that her body was changing fast to accommodate the growing baby inside her, and the tiredness was getting more pronounced. She sighed and sat back on the bench. The sun was hot, and she was thirsty. She wished she had brought some water with her. "That was dumb of me," she thought. She closed her eyes for a minute and leaned back on the bench. The warm sun bathed her face and she felt comforted by it. She would just sit and wait.

She must have dozed off. She could hear a horn honking and the voice of a man speaking Italian. The man's voice was getting closer. She forced herself to open her eyes and looked up, adjusting her eyes to the sun. The man approached her saying something. "Checosa?" Rena said hoping that was the right thing to say.

"Rena, ci fai qui?"

187

Rena? Who was it? Rena shook herself and sat up properly, shielding her eyes so she could see the man. Her heart sank. There, right in front of her, was Zio Augusto.

"Oh," said Rena shocked to see him. "It's okay, I'm taking the bus," said Rena unaware that she was using her hands to shoo him away.

"Come with me," Zio Augusto said slowly in heavily accented English.

"No gracie," said Rena, "I'm going to take the bus."

Zio Augusto shook his head. "Non, bella, non, come with me," he said again gently holding out his hand with a small smile.

He looked so concerned and fatherly that all Rena's resolve dissolved and she burst into tears. "Oh Uncle Augusto," she cried, "Everything is terrible," she wailed.

Zio Augusto came and sat down with her on the bench and got out a tissue from his pocket. Rena took it and wiped her tears. She looked at Zio Augusto. "I can't go with you," she said. "I have to go home," she said sadly looking down at her hands that were crumpling the tissue.

Zio Augusto looked at her and sighed. He paused for a moment as if he was thinking about something, and then nodded. "I take you to Roma," he said.

"What?" Rena asked surprised.

"Zio Augusto take you," he said grabbing her suitcase. Rena sat on the bench, shocked. "Venire bella, venire," he said gesturing towards his Fiat.

The drive to Rome was as beautiful as she had remembered on the way from it, and Rena gazed at the beauty of the surrounding countryside as Zio Augusto's Fiat sped along. She couldn't believe he was doing this for her and his kindness brought tears to her eyes. She wished she could speak to him to let him know how much this meant to her, but words wouldn't be enough, even if she could speak Italian. She had decided last night to go back to Toronto. She would have had been forced to at some point anyway, and Italy was just too painful for her now. She knew that running away didn't solve anything but she had to go. Carl didn't believe her, and even Anna and Falcone had questioned the truth in what she was saying. She needed to get away. She needed to go home.

They drove for two hours in silence and then suddenly Zio Augusto pulled into a service center at the side of the highway. He went into the service center store while Rena stood outside the car to stretch her legs. When he came back out, Zio Augusto handed her a bottle of water and Rena took it eagerly and drank the cool liquid quickly. She hadn't realized how parched she was. She gestured to Zio Augusto that she was going to go to the washroom and walked in the center. When she came out there was another bottle for her. "Gracie," Rena said taking the bottle and smiling at Zio Augusto. She got back into the Fiat and Zio Augusto smiled at her. He nodded. "Si," he said.

"Si," said Rena smiling back. He was kind.

They continued on the road and stopped again an hour later and had meat and cheese sandwiches that Zio Augusto had purchased. Rena was hungry and appreciated the food. She hadn't thought this far ahead when she had left and had neglected to see that she had no cash in her purse. They arrived at Ciampino airport in Rome an hour later. Zio Augusto tried to come in with Rena, but she firmly told him no and thanked him for helping her. He gave her a big hug and then kissed her on both cheeks.

"Sicuro bella di viaggio," he said. "Safe," he said.

Rena turned around and walked into the airport. She looked back and saw him watching her get to the departure lounge to buy her ticket. When she had got her ticket, she turned around again to have a look. He had left.

***

Carl and Falcone got to Anna's house an hour later. Anna didn't seem to be home yet from her errands so Falcone let himself in with a key she had hidden above the door. He called out for Rena but they heard nothing. "She must have gone with Anna," Falcone said. "We'll wait. Falcone went into the kitchen and Carl followed. He grabbed two soft drinks from the fridge and the guys went outside in the backyard to wait. Carl felt anxious. His last meeting with Rena hadn't gone well, and she had asked him to leave. He hoped that they could have a calmer discussion today. He took a sip of the soft drink Falcone gave him. It helped soothe his parched mouth. He was nervous, and it didn't help that he had a hangover. He could kick himself for drinking like that.

Falcone started asking Carl about baseball and soon the two of them were deep into a back and forth discussion on their favourite teams. That is how Anna saw them when she arrived home. She came into the house with bags full of shopping and went to the counter to drop them off. She heard Falcone and Carl outside and took a quick peak. "I will go outside once I put the groceries away," she thought. After putting everything in its place, Anna grabbed herself a bottle of water and walked to the back door, opening it leaning her head out. "Hey guys, I see that you have helped yourself to my fridge," she said. Neither of them noticed. "Hey GUYS!" she yelled catching Falcone so off guard that he almost fell off his chair.

"Woah, cousin, chill," he said jokingly.

"You guys must have been talking about something good to not hear me the first time," Anna said walking up to them.

"Baseball," said Carl smiling.

"Ah, just baseball," Anna said nodding.

"*Just* baseball?" Falcone said. "That is blasphemy!" he retorted sounding affronted.

Anna laughed. "Please," she said shaking her head, "I didn't even know you knew that word Falcone," she said laughing.

Falcone picked up a stick and pretended to throw it at her. "Hey, don't forget whose house you are in," Anna said laughing and ducking.

Anna sat down on a chair beside Carl. "So, how are things, Carl, did you talk to Rena?" she asked. Carl looked surprised.

"No, we were waiting for you guys to get back," he said.

"Rena didn't come with me," Anna said confused. "She's not here?"

"I called out for her," Falcone said, "But nobody answered."

"Maybe she is taking a nap," said Anna, "Although it is past two, but she might have been tired." "Let me go check on her," she said getting up and walking into the house.

"I thought she was with her," Falcone said looking apologetically at Carl. "Sorry buddy, if I had known she was here you guys could have been working things out by now."

"Don't worry about it," said Carl, "I thought she was with Anna too," he said starting to get a bad feeling. He took another swig of the soft drink. Something didn't feel right. He turned to look as Anna walked out of the house holding something in her hand. She looked pale. "Anna," Carl said standing up.

"She's gone," she said bursting into tears.

Carl took the letter from Anna's shaking hands while Falcone got up to help Anna to a seat. "Where did she go?" he asked Anna.

"To the airport," said Carl reading the letter quickly. "I've got to go there now," he said urgently to Falcone.

"I know," said Falcone getting up, "but what did she say?"

"That she is heading back to Toronto because she needs to make some decisions," said Carl paraphrasing the letter.

"Yah and she also says how hurt she is that nobody believes her, especially her best friend," wailed Anna. "I have been terrible, I wasn't supportive."

"I don't think she really meant it Anna," Falcone said reassuringly. "I'll call the airport to see when the flights to Toronto are, Carl you call or text her to see where she is," Falcone said taking charge and dashing into the house to check Anna's computer. Anna followed him in and stood over him as he searched the flights on her computer. "Crap," Falcone said.

"I can't get hold of her, what is it?" asked Carl coming to the room looking at his friend.

"The last flight to Toronto leaves in less than an hour," Falcone said looking up at him.

Carl was horrified. There was no way they could make it to the airport on time. His worst fears had been realized. She was gone.

CHAPTER 33

Rena walked out of the plane onto the gate smiling quickly at the pilot on the way out. She was drained and exhausted. The flight had been a bit turbulent but Rena had been too tired from the events of the last day to care. She felt nauseous and figured it was from the pregnancy and the time change. She wanted to quickly get her luggage and a cab and go home. Home. "That is a funny word," she thought. She had left Toronto originally because she had felt trapped and stifled, and now she was running back. *To what?* She got through customs quickly and waited at the baggage carousel for her luggage. She just wanted to get her bags and get out of here. She needed to get somewhere where she could be alone and cry. She finally saw her bag and went to reach for it. An elderly man reached forward and got it for her. "Thanks," she said smiling wanly at the man.

"You're welcome sweetie," he said.

Rena wanted to cry, Carl had called her sweetie a few times, and she had loved it. She could feel the tears well up in her eyes. She couldn't cry she had to be strong; she needed to be for this baby. She thanked the man again and wheeled her bag out into the Arrivals lounge. She could see the excited faces of families coming to pick up their relatives and friends. "There is nobody to pick me up," she thought sighing. She remembered her first meeting with Uncle Augusto in the Rome airport. It seemed like years ago. She walked as quickly as she could through the crowds and got to the street. She was approached right away by a cabbie, and was happy to let him help her with her suitcase. She climbed into the back seat of the cab and closed her eyes. She was home.

Half an hour later, she stood at the door of the apartment that she and Jarod had shared during their marriage. The cabbie had offered to walk her to her door, but had refused. She needed to take her time with this. She walked slowly into the building to the elevator. She looked around the lobby. It looked bigger than she had remembered it. *Cleaner.* That thought might have made her laugh once, but Rena was too tired to think of that. The elevator door opened and Rena wheeled her suitcase in. The door closed and Rena pushed the button for the fourth floor. As the elevator started moving up, Rena could feel her stomach churn. She had never liked elevators. The elevator door opened and Rena got out. She walked down the hallway to the end and stood in front of the apartment door where she and Jarod had lived. She was expecting to feel guilt, regret, anger, but the only thing she felt was sadness. She put her key in the door to the apartment, opened it, and walked in. It was still light out so she could see clearly. The apartment looked spacious and felt airy. Rena had never remembered it feeling airy; she had always felt trapped and smothered in it. She walked around looking at her things and sat down on the couch. She didn't feel trapped anymore.

At that moment, she realized something. Something Carl had told her, about forgiveness. The thought of Carl brought intense pain to her heart, but she was willing to give it a try. "Jarod, I forgive you, I let you go," she said aloud. She sat there for a while, breathing in the space. She finally understood what Carl had meant. She had forgiven Jarod, and she felt free, freer than she had in ages. She stayed on the couch, letting go the pain of the past, and releasing the tears that were begging to flow down her face.

The room was starting to get darker. Rena sighed and got up from the couch and went to get her cell phone. She needed to call to get her utilities turned back on. When Anna had invited her to Italy, she had got them turned off since she wasn't sure how long she would stay there. But she was back now, and pregnant. She needed to have hot water and electricity. She searched on her phone, located the number of the utility company, and punched in the numbers. The customer service agent at the other end of the line answered and took her information and asked her to hold the line.

Rena moved around the apartment while she was waiting, taking stock of all the things she had to do. She looked in her kitchen cupboards, found crackers, and a few granola bars. That would suffice until she could get out to get some shopping. The phone crackled and the agent came back on the line.

"Mam?" the voice asked.

"Yes," Rena said.

"Your water and electricity were turned on this morning," she said.

"What?" asked Rena.

"Your utilities are on Mam," the agent said again.

"But I didn't call to get that done; that is strange," Rena said walking to the wall and reaching for the light switch. Sure enough, as she flipped the switch the light turned on. "Oh, the lights are working," Rena said surprised. She moved to the sink and turned on the tap. The pipes made a loud banging noise and murky water came out of the spout. Rena left the water running and soon it was clear. "Well that's strange, the water works too, but I didn't call," she said.

"Well from the notes here it looks like someone called this morning and asked that it be hooked up immediately," she said.

"Oh, that is so strange since I only arrived back in Canada a couple of hours ago," Rena said.

"Let me see what I can find here," said the agent. "Usually a quick reinstatement has an additional fee."

"Yah that I figured," said Rena.

"Okay," the agent said, "I see here that the fee and monthly payment was charged to an outside account."

"Really?" asked Rena surprised.

"Yes, three months was paid in full."

"That is really strange," said Rena.

"I can look into it more and get back to you Mam," the clerk said.

"Sure that would be great," said Rena. She thanked the clerk and hung up the call. It was strange, but Rena wasn't about to look a gift horse in the mouth. Now that she had water, she was going to take a shower.

Thirty minutes later, she was in the kitchen making a list of items she needed from the store. She grabbed her purse and a granola bar and left the apartment to go shopping.

CHAPTER 34

A week had passed and Rena finally felt like she was beginning to settle back into the apartment. The morning nausea had tamed a bit and Rena felt like her mornings were beginning to function a lot better. She turned to look at her house line and cell phone. Anna had called many times since she had returned and Rena had not picked up the phone. She wasn't ready to talk to anybody. She wanted to get her life in order so she could take care of her baby. And right now, that did not include fixing issues with her friends. Carl had called her cell phone and texted a few times as well, but Rena had ignored it. Unless he was getting tested, she could not talk to him. She still felt hurt that he had not believed her, and a part of her realized where he was coming from. But she had to move on. The last week had given her a strength and fierceness like she had never felt before. She had to protect and take care of her baby and herself. Today she had an appointment with an obstetrician to make sure the pregnancy was progressing healthily. That was what was important. She swallowed the empty feeling of sadness that she felt when thinking of Carl. Her heart ached, but she couldn't acknowledge it. She had to put it to the back of her mind.

Thinking of Carl and the situation made her feel restless and uneasy, so Rena decided to go for a walk before the appointment to calm her nerves. She wasn't sure why she was feeling this way. She had been taking care of herself since she had found out she was pregnant, so there should be nothing to worry about. As she walked out of the building and towards the local park, she breathed in the fresh air deeply. "Relax, Rena," she thought to herself, "Relax." A few minutes later though, the feeling of uneasiness came back, and this time it felt worse. Her stomach had a dull ache and she felt dizzy. Rena quickly turned around in the park and started walking back to the apartment. She felt desperate to lie down. When she got through her door, she went right to the couch to lie down and took a few deep slow breaths. She started to feel a bit better but then felt like she had to get up. She slowly got up off the couch and made her way to the bathroom. Maybe I am just off after flying and have a bug," she thought. She went to the bathroom, sat down, and sighed. It felt better to sit this way. She looked down and then she noticed it. Blood.

Rena was frightened. The more she wiped the more blood she saw. She had heard about early miscarriages but this couldn't be happening to her. She started to panic. This baby was all she had left of Carl. All she had in the world. Distraught, she got up from the toilet and quickly grabbed her phone and dialed Anna. Anna answered on the second ring.

"Rena, how are you, I have been trying to get a hold of you for a week now," Anna said sounding anxious and upset.

"Anna," Rena wailed.

"What's wrong?" Anna said turning from sounding annoyed to sounding worried. "Rena what is wrong?"

"T-the baby, Anna, there's blood, Anna I'm scared," she cried into the phone.

"Oh shit, Rena," Anna said.

Rena felt sick; she couldn't lose this baby. She started to feel dizzy and sat back down.

"Rena, are you there?" Anna said on the line.

"Yes."

"Rena, call 911, call now," Anna said.

"Anna please help," Rena pleaded.

"Rena, you have to hang up and call 911, please," said Anna.

"Okay," said Rena, "can I call you back?"

"Yes," said Anna, "but hang up now Rena," she said.

Rena hung up. Tears were streaming down her face. She felt a dull pain in her abdomen. "Oh please, please don't go," she cried talking to her unborn child. She turned her phone over and tapped in 911.

The call to 911 had quick results. Within ten minutes, an ambulance arrived and Rena was placed on a stretcher. The attendees asked her all kinds of questions but Rena could only think of her baby. They arrived at the hospital fifteen minutes later, and the attendees unloaded Rena and moved her quickly into the Emergency department of the hospital. Nurses surrounded her right away and she was whisked to a private area of the ward. A nurse came in and asked Rena more questions. How long was her pregnancy, who was her obstetrician, and who was her emergency contact? Rena couldn't think. When Jarod had died she had a lost a lot of her friends. But they hadn't been her friends anyway. Jarod had consumed her life, and she had lost all of the previous friends she had had except Anna. His parents had been so distraught at his death that even looking at her at devastated them, so she had given up having any contact. Her own parents had died years before and she had no siblings. She gave the nurse Anna's details, and asked again if her baby would be okay. The nurse smiled wanly at her and told her to wait for the doctor to examine her. Another nurse came in and got Rena undressed and into a hospital gown. She then put an IV into Rena's arm. She was gentle, friendly and reminded Rena of the mother figures she had seen on popular television shows. "It's okay dear," she said, "we'll get you and this baby all fixed up," she said.

Somehow, this comforted Rena and she started to relax a bit, resting back down on the hospital bed. What seemed like hours later, but was probably only ten minutes, a tall middle-aged doctor came into the room. He pulled the curtains across to give Rena privacy. "Hello Rena," he said looking at her chart. "You are pregnant and bleeding," he said, "how far are you along?"

Rena explained to him that she hadn't seen anyone yet and that she was probably a couple of months pregnant.

"Well, we will have a look and figure it out," he said. The nurse put the stirrups up at the end of bed and instructed Rena to put her feet on either pad. The doctor had just started his examination when another nurse popped her head in behind the curtain.

"The father is here," she said.

Rena started. The father? The heart started to pound and beat wildly. Carl was here. The doctor looked up at Rena.

"Do you want him in here?"

"Yes," said Rena looking anxiously at the curtains. The nurse parted the curtains and in walked Falcone.

Rena burst into tears. Falcone quickly rushed to her side and held her hand. "It's okay Rena," he said, taking her hand in his.

"W-when did you get here?" she asked.

"Two days ago Rena, I should have called but I wasn't sure you would want to see me," he said. "I was a jerk," he whispered into her ear.

"I thought it was…," Rena said and stopped midway in her sentence. The doctor had started examining Rena and she jumped when he touched her cervix.

"It looks okay," said the doctor. "Your cervix is closed, and the bleeding has stopped. It is common in early pregnancy to have some bleeding and some women bleed all throughout."

"Thank god," said Rena relieved.

"To be safe though," the doctor said, "I want to keep you overnight and you have strict orders to rest for the next couple of days, no marathons, nothing crazy," he said looking sternly at her.

"Okay," said Rena nodding in affirmation. The doctor left and she sighed. If taking care of herself and her baby was causing her body stress, she was in trouble.

"It's okay Rena, I'll be here for you," Falcone said sensing her distress.

Rena nodded. She knew he would, she should have

realized that; but it was Carl she wished had been there; it was Carl she wished could have said those words. "I know Falcone, thanks," she said meaning it.

Falcone put her hands to his lips and kissed them. "Rena, why did you leave?" he asked. Rena sighed. She knew at some point she would be confronted by this, and had taken time to think about it. "You can tell me Rena, I won't say anything to Carl, or Anna or anyone," Falcone said. Rena looked at her friend. He had always teased her and flirted with her, but deep down she knew he was a kind and generous person. Rena knew it was time to let go of the past. She sighed again.

"I wanted to leave Jarod for so long Falcone," she said. "But I felt scared and as time went on I felt like I couldn't go on without him, and then I resented him and myself for being stuck in that situation." Falcone looked at her.

"Rena, nobody was fooled. Even Anna will tell you, we all knew you weren't happy. You disappeared."

"I know," said Rena. "But when Jarod died I felt free and alive again, and I vowed I would never let anyone take my power away again. So when Carl kept wanting to get me to say something that wasn't true, I couldn't let it destroy me, I had to leave," she said a tear falling down her cheek.

"I know Rena, I know," Falcone said wiping away her tear. "Anna freaked out when you left; she said we were too hard on you. She even yelled at Carl, and told him to get tested, that he was acting like a baby and that you didn't have a dishonest bone in your body," Falcone said.

Rena giggled. She could see Anna losing her temper and telling the boys off. "Good Anna, I love you," she thought.

"I left the next day Rena," he said. "Carl had to stay to finish up some of the training we had to do. He wanted to come badly. He has a lot to work out Rena. He never told you, did he?" he asked.

"That he couldn't have kids?" she asked. "No that didn't come up, ever," said Rena.

"But he didn't tell you what happened to him, with the other woman he met after his wife."

"No," said Rena.

"Rena she-."

Rena interrupted him. She was exhausted and this was too much for her to absorb. She wasn't sure she wanted to know anything now. She just wanted her baby to be well and get on with her life.

"Falc, please don't," she said touching his arm to stop him. "I need to rest," she said giving him a small smile.

"Okay Rena, but you really should know," he said seriously.

"I know, just not yet," Rena said. If there was anything she needed to know, it had to be from Carl.

"Okay, I will go," he said kissing her forehead and moving to leave. "By the way," he said turning to look at her, "I have now seen a lot more of you than I ever imagined. Anytime you want to have a go Rena," he said grinning mischievously.

"You know how to kill a moment Falcone," Rena said throwing a pillow at him as he ducked out of the curtains. Rena lay back on her pillow and laughed. Falcone could always make her smile. She closed her eyes. It had been a stressful day; she needed to relax.

CHAPTER 35

Carl sat in the waiting room. He had been here before. The clinic smelled medicinal and was full of other men like him, some couples, some not, all eagerly waiting to start a process to see if they were fertile or not. He leaned forward, his arms on his thighs. He wasn't sure why he was here. He knew this was a futile exercise. He almost felt stupid being here. But he had to do this, if only to prove it to her. She had given him no choice. But then what? That was the question that burned in his mind, and had caused him many sleepless nights. What then? He had played many scenarios in his head over the past weeks, but all of them came down to the same result. He could not let her go. He didn't want to let her go. He sighed his shoulders releasing. He felt a hand pat him on the back.

"It's okay Carl, you can do this," Matt said.

Carl turned his head to look at his brother. "Yah?" he asked, feeling unsure.

Matt nodded. "You can," he said firmly.

"Thank God for Matt," thought Carl. He couldn't have

done this without him. "Yah," Carl replied nodding to himself.

When Matt had heard the news from Italy about Rena, there had been silence on the phone. Carl had at first thought that they had lost the connection. "Matt are you still there?" he had asked.

"Yes, Carl I am shocked," he said, "I honestly don't know what to say."

"She wants me to get tested, like I don't know the result of that," Carl said sarcastically. "She won't even talk to me."

"What are you going to do?" Matt asked gently.

Carl sighed. "What can I do? I just want her to be honest. Why do I have to go through this again?"

"I don't know Carl, I just don't know. I am surprised. I only met her the one time, but she didn't strike me as someone to be dishonest."

"I know I know," Carl said. "Ah Matt, what should I do?"

"I can't answer that for you Carl," Matt replied.

"I know," Carl said again, "I just wish you could, it would be easier."

"Whatever you decide I am here for you, you know that," said Matt consolingly.

"Thanks Matt, I don't know what I would do without you." Carl had realized that the only way to talk to Rena was to do what she asked, but he needed Matt's support. And that was why they were here, in the clinic, waiting with everyone else. But being here in this clinic brought back a lot of memories he wanted to forget.

"Carl," the nurse at the desk stood up and called bringing him back to the present. Carl walked up to the desk.

"Thanks Janice," he said giving her a half smile. Janice had been a staple at the clinic in all the years that Carl had gone there. About 60 years old, Janice was a firecracker and kept things at the clinic light. She was a comforting presence and Carl was happy she was still there.

"Enjoy," Janice said winking at him as she passed him a magazine and bottle.

"I'll be thinking of you," Carl joked as he walked to the room.

"Wouldn't want it any other way darling," said Janice hooting with laughter.

***

This time she didn't say much. There were long periods of silence. If she didn't talk, nobody would. He didn't know what to say to her. He didn't know what to ask her. He didn't know how to love her. "He didn't, but I do," the voice said. The dark brown eyes penetrated her dream. "I will always love you, I will always be here for you," the voice said. "You will never feel alone again. Ever."

Rena woke up in the hospital bed. She wriggled around. She was surprised at how rested she felt. It was the first full night of sleep she had had since coming back from Italy. She felt calm and relaxed. It was an odd feeling considering all that she had been through. "Maybe it's because the baby is okay and I know I can go home today," she thought. The nurse entered her room.

"Good morning," she said.

"Good morning," said Rena trying to sit up.

"How are you feeling," asked the nurse.

"Actually really good, I haven't slept this well in ages," Rena said smiling.

"That's good to hear," said the nurse getting out her stethoscope. "I am going to take your vitals," she said, "anymore bleeding this morning?"

"I haven't checked yet," said Rena.

"Okay we will check it out," the nurse said getting ready to check her blood pressure. Fifteen minutes later the nurse had finished. "Everything looks good," she said. "No more bleeding. You should be able to go home once Dr. Caspers does his rounds.

"Oh great," said Rena.

"Should I call your boyfriend?" the nurse asked.

"My boyfriend?" Rena asked surprised. "Oh, you mean," Rena giggled. "I will call him, but thanks," she said grinning. The thought of Falcone being her boyfriend was hysterical.

The nurse left and Rena got up slowly. *Your boyfriend.* Rena picked up her phone on the nightstand. The texts from Carl had stopped a few days ago. Even though she had been annoyed with him for being so relentless, she had counted on those texts as a glimmer of hope that he would come around and everything would be okay. But they had stopped. She looked at her phone. Nothing. A feeling of anxiety hit her. She wasn't sure she could do this alone. She had no time to dwell on those thoughts however, as at that moment the doctor came in to look at her. He was tall and grey-haired and looked close to sixty.

"How are you doing?" he asked in a booming voice, picking up her chart at the end of the bed and reading it, not looking at her.

"Okay," said Rena quietly.

The nurse from the morning came in. "Vitals are good and the bleeding has stopped," she told the doctor.

The doctor looked up from the chart and glanced at Rena. "Let's take a quick look," he said peering over his reading glasses.

Rena lay back and the doctor examined her. "Looks good," he said. "The bleeding has stopped. You need to take it easy for a few days. Where is the father?" he asked looking at the chart again.

"Uh-h," Rena sputtered.

He looked up again over his glasses. "He's where?" he asked.

"He's uh away for work," she said. "It's not really lying," she thought, Carl was in Italy, working. The nurse gave her a look.

"You need someone to make sure you stay off your feet for a couple of days. Is there anyone like that?" the doctor asked.

"Uh – h –h," Rena wracked her brain.

She could tell the doctor was getting impatient. "He must have a ton of other patients to look at," she thought. "I g-guess, I can find someone," she said.

The doctor seemed annoyed and handed the chart to the nurse. "She can't leave unless someone is here who promises to take care of her, otherwise she stays," he said. "I want you to make sure," he said to the nurse who nodded. He glanced back at Rena. "The father should be here. It's not enough to donate the sperm," he said sternly.

Rena felt chastened. She wasn't sure what to say. The doctor glared at her and walked out of the room. "It's not my fault," thought Rena. She turned back to the nurse who was standing by the bed.

"Can I call someone for you?" she asked.

"It's okay, I'll call my friend," Rena said. The nurse looked at her like she didn't believe her. "Great," Rena thought.

"Okay, I will need to talk to him before you can go," she said firmly.

"Okay," said Rena trying to sound confident.

The nurse left the room and Rena stared at her phone. She loved Falcone, he was good friend, but there was no way he would look after her for two days. She would be waiting hand on foot after him; it was just the way Falcone was. Rena started to panic. She would be stuck in the hospital. What if they never let her go? She had to get Falcone to lie for her. She called Falcone's number. There was no answer. She left a message on his line letting him know that they wouldn't let her leave if he couldn't watch her for two days and that he had to lie for her so she could leave. She sat back on the bed and rested her head on the pillow. "He better pull through for me," she thought.

CHAPTER 36

This time he was there alone. He had been called early this morning to come back into the clinic to give another sample. "It is odd," thought Carl. He had never had to do this before. He sighed. Matt had offered to come but Carl was a big boy, he could do this on his own. Janice glanced at him from behind the desk and smiled.

"You just can't keep away from me, can you," she said grinning at him.

"I would be here every day if they would let me," Carl said responding with a cheeky grin.

Janice laughed. "You and everyone else," she said waving her hand around the room at the grinning faces.

"I'll take a number," said Carl listening to the chuckles in the room.

"Well your number is up," said Janice beckoning him with a cup and magazine.

"I could only be so lucky," Carl said taking the items

and giving her a kiss on the cheek. He could hear Janice's laugh as he walked down the hall to the room.

***

Rena was stressed. She had called and texted Falcone a few times but he hadn't answered his phone or texted back. "Where are you Falcone?" she thought. He had promised the other day to be there for her, and now he was gone. "Typical," Rena thought. She got up out of the hospital bed and grabbed her clothes. She would get dressed and washed and then hopefully Falcone would call back. The dietary aid came in with a breakfast tray and put it on the table beside Rena's bed. "Thanks," said Rena eyeing the food. It didn't look great. Some porridge muck, toast, and jam, a banana and an orange juice. She picked up the porridge to give it a sniff and her stomach growled. "Okay, I'll eat first and then get dressed," she decided sitting down and grabbing a spoonful of the porridge.

Half an hour later she was back sitting on the bed, dressed, washed, fed, and ready to go. She checked her phone again. *Falcone, where are you?* The nurse who she saw in the morning came in.

"All ready to go?" she asked smiling.

"Yes," said Rena, "But my friend hasn't called back."

"I just spoke to him, dear," the nurse said smiling. "He should be with you in a little bit, he had a friend to visit here as well," she said.

"Oh," said Rena wondering whom Falcone could be visiting.

She sat in the chair next to the bed and sighed with relief. "Thanks Falcone, I knew you wouldn't let me down," she thought.

She could hear the nurse outside the room, "She's all ready for you," the nurse said.

She could hear the man's voice as he entered the room with her. Rena looked up ready to see Falcone, and was shocked at what she saw. It wasn't Falcone.

"Hi Rena, remember me?" asked Matt reaching out his hand to shake hers.

Rena stuttered in surprise. "H-hi," she said fully expecting to see Carl come in.

"I hope you don't mind," said Matt smiling fondly at her.

Rena looked at his kind eyes. They reminded her of Carl and pain hit her heart. "Um, no, it's fine," she said, not sure what to say.

"How are you feeling?" he asked.

"Fine, good," said Rena looking toward the door.

Matt turned to look at the door. "He's not here Rena," he said gently.

Tears welled in Rena's eyes.

"Listen," said Matt, "I don't want to get involved with what is going on, it is between you and Carl, but for whatever its worth, I know my brother loves you and would have done anything he could to be here for you." Rena started to open her mouth and Matt held up his hand. "But," he said, "I'm not here to talk to you about that Rena."

"Why are you here?" asked Rena.

"I'm here to make sure you are okay, and to take you home," he said.

"Oh, Falcone is coming to get me," Rena said assuredly.

"We've had an emergency downtown and he had to stay, he asked me to get you safely home," Matt said.

"Okay," said Rena confused. She had told Falcone she could not be alone, but she guessed he hadn't heard her. "It is better anyways," thought Rena. She was on the verge of tears and knew the minute Matt dropped her off at her apartment the floodgates would open.

"As long as it is no trouble," she said to the tall smiling man in front of her.

"No trouble at all," said Matt looking at her kindly.

And then it struck her. "He believes me," thought Rena. *Carl's brother believes me.*

They drove in silence for most of the way to Rena's apartment. Matt had started off talking a bit about his kids and his family but got quiet once Rena didn't respond. Now that she was going home, Rena didn't feel as relaxed as she had upon waking in the morning. The stress of the last week was coming back, and Rena knew the road ahead alone wasn't going to be easy. She took a deep breath in and exhaled slowly. She would be okay; she had to be.

"Everything all right Rena?" Matt asked breaking her thoughts.

Rena turned to him with a small smile. "Yah," she said, "Just thinking of all the things I have to do."

"Rena if you need any help, anything at all, you can call me okay?" Matt said.

"He's sincere," thought Rena; she could hear it in his voice. "Thanks, Matt," she replied and meant it.

They arrived on Rena's street and Matt drove into the building complex visitors parking. "Um, you can just drop me off if you want," said Rena.

"No, I have strict instructions to get you safely inside," Matt said winking at her.

Rena smiled to herself. "It is too bad that there is this circumstance between us, if it had been different we could have been great friends," Rena thought. They got out of Matt's car and Matt walked over to Rena's door to let her out. He got her bags and they walked to the front door of the building where Matt held the door for Rena to go through. At the elevator, he held the door again so Rena could get on. "That's where Carl gets his chivalry from," thought Rena.

They arrived on her floor and Rena walked to her apartment door. She could smell something coming from her door. It smelled familiar. Rena opened the door to her apartment and no sooner did she step into the apartment a mass of black flowing hair and the strong scent of Dolce & Gabbana perfume permeated her senses, and she found herself being given a big bear hug. "Rena," cried Anna. "I am so glad you and the baby are okay," she said tears in her eyes. "I was so worried, I could not get here fast enough," she said.

"Oh Anna, thanks so much," said Rena elated at seeing her friend, and returning the hug and not letting go. "Thank-you," she said again tears streaming down her face.

"I'll take good care of you Rena," Anna said, "Don't worry, you and this baby will be fine," she said determinedly.

Rena nodded and held Anna tighter. She needed her friend. She felt her heart was going to break all over again. "Oh, Matt," Rena said, remembering Carl's brother and starting to pull away from Anna.

"It's okay Rena," Anna said hugging her close, "He ducked out."

The tears flooded Rena's eyes. "Oh Anna, what have I done?" she said wiping back the tears that were streaming down her face. "All I ever wanted is love, and Carl loves me, and I have been pushing him away. I am upset that he didn't believe me, but I know why, and I should have been more understanding," she wailed.

"Rena, its okay, its okay," Anna said consoling her.

"No, it isn't," said Rena pushing away. "I love him and I let him go."

"Listen to me Rena, you did the best you could with the information you had at the time, it's okay," Anna stated again.

"How can it be?" asked Rena, "When the man I love, the father of my baby isn't with me?"

"Forgive yourself Rena, it is all okay, you were doing what was best at the time, and personally I still think he was a jerk for reacting the way he did," Anna said angrily.

She sounded so annoyed that Rena giggled. "Really?" she said looking at her friend.

"Really Rena. If I see him I will probably clock him one," she said adamantly. Rena laughed. "We can do this Rena, together," said Anna.

"But what about Simon?" asked Rena, "He must not be happy that I took you away again," she said remorsefully.

"He's not back until next week," said Anna, "and we'll figure it out, don't worry," she said giving Rena another big squeeze. "Now com'on girl," Anna said rolling her 'r's, "I have some bread in the oven for you. We'll talk about the rest after you've eaten," she said leading Rena to the kitchen.

CHAPTER 37

Matt walked into the police division. It was chaos. The commotion downtown had caused nearly every police officer in the city to be called into duty. A group of university students had been reveling at a keg party and it had got out of hand. Over 3000 students had caused a raucous and several divisions had been called in to help. Carl saw Matt come in and pushed his way through the throng of students waiting to be questioned, booked and fingerprinted.

"Matt, did you see her?" he asked his brother. "Is she okay?"

"Yes, I saw her, she's okay, scared, but the baby's fine," he said pushing through with Carl to the back office. They got into the office and Carl closed the door.

"She's okay though, right?" Carl asked concerned. He had freaked out when he heard that Rena was in the hospital. He wanted to go there so badly, but Rena had told him she didn't want to see him until he was tested. Carl didn't have any results yet, so he didn't want to upset her or the baby.

"She's fine, and Anna's here to look after her, so she is in good hands for now," said Matt looking at his younger brother. "Carl, you are going to have to make some decisions," he said.

"I know," Carl said sighing and looking at the floor. "I love her Matt," he said looking up at the older brother he adored. "I cannot imagine having a life without her," he said. "It would be too painful."

"Then you will have to figure out what you will do when the results come in," Matt said. "Just in case, you should really examine how you feel," he said looking at Carl with all of the understanding and compassion an older brother could give.

"I know how I feel," Carl said. "I just don't know how Rena feels anymore. I feel like a jerk, and I don't even know the results yet," he said leaning back to grab the phone on the desk that was ringing. "Hello," Carl said in an authoritative tone. "Oh, yes, hi Janice. Sure, but can't I just find out over the phone? Yes, I know, I get it, yes, okay see you then," he said hanging up the phone. "The results are in, I will find out tomorrow."

"Okay, tomorrow then," said Matt walking to him and patting him on the back. "Let's go get some answers about this rave," he said nodding to the throng outside the door.

"Let's go," said Carl following him out.

***

Carl woke up the next morning with a terrific headache. "Ow," he verbalized loudly moving his head from the pillow. His head felt heavy and his body ached. "Ugh," he said trying to get up and landing back down on the pillow. He felt awful. The night before had ended late, but Carl had felt fine afterwards. Maybe a little tired and anxious, but he knew he had a big day the next morning, so the anxiety was normal and to be expected. But this morning he felt terrible. He lifted his hand to his forehead. He felt warm but who knew. "This could not have happened at a worst time," he thought. With resolve, he lifted up his head and sat on the side of the bed. His head banged like a jackhammer and he thought he was going to be sick. "Great," he thought, "Just great." He ambled slowly to the shower and his legs felt heavy like concrete blocks. "Damn," he thought. He walked into the bathroom and opened the medicine cabinet to take out the thermometer. He probably was the only male his age that had one, but he had got used to watching his temperature when he had lymphoma, and never got out of the habit. He put the thermometer in his ear and took it out. "Shit," he said aloud. He definitely had a fever. He grabbed the ibuprofen from the cabinet and took two. "Hopefully this will help the fever and this headache to subside," he thought. He walked slowly back to his bedside table and picked up this phone to call the clinic. After talking with the answering service, Carl ambled back to the bathroom and turned on the shower. He knew they weren't going to let him into the clinic today. Not with this fever. He started to get in the shower and just made it to the toilet bowl before he got sick.

***

The brown eyes stared at her and penetrated her brain. She could feel the depth of the eyes… they went down into her soul. "I love you, I love you, I need you," they said. Her heart ached; she tried to cry out. She wanted to say, "I love you too, I love you, I need you, come to me," but the words wouldn't come out. The brown eyes started fading way and then they disappeared. "No, NO!" she tried to cry out. "Don't leave, I love you, I love you." But they left; and she felt lost and alone.

Rena woke up feeling a little nauseous. She hadn't felt nauseous in a couple of days and the feeling disappointed her. Her stomach was in knots and she felt nervous. Something about a dream. She knew she should remember it, but she couldn't, and she had a sick feeling in her stomach that she knew wasn't from the nausea. Carl. She grabbed her phone from the side table. There were no messages, no calls. For the first time Rena had the realization that maybe he would never call. She felt shaky as she walked to the bathroom. Anna could console her all she wanted, but she would never get over this. She turned on the shower and stepped in. At least the running water would hide the sound of her cries.

CHAPTER 38

Carl sat in the waiting room and tried to read the magazine. He couldn't concentrate. It had been five days since the clinic had called him about his results, and Carl had been unable to go. He had been sick for four days, and then the weekend had come and the clinic was closed. Now he couldn't wait to find out. He needed to know; and had waited too long. He laughed inwardly. The sickness must have made him crazy, because even he was thinking now that maybe this child could be is. He shook his head. "Best prepare for the inevitable," he thought. Janice called to him from the desk.

"Okay sweetheart, your turn," she pointed to him and gestured to the office door.

"You want me to come?" Matt asked beside him.

"Yes," said Carl, "Yes, let's go."

The men walked into the doctor's office and Carl walked over to the doctor and accepted his outstretched hand.

"Hello Dr. Farber," he said.

"Carl, good to see you," Doctor Farber said.

"Matt," he said shaking Matt's hand. "Let's sit down and talk," he said gesturing to the seats on the other side of his desk.

Carl and Matt sat down on the seats while the doctor picked up a file. "Here we go," thought Carl apprehensively.

"So Carl as you know we conducted two tests this time, 24 hours apart," Doctor Farber started.

"Yes, that was different," said Carl nodding in affirmation.

"Yes," said Dr. Farber. "We needed to be sure of the results. I know this has been an incredibly stressful time for you. We have been here before," Dr. Farber said looking at Carl. Carl could feel his heart sink. The doctor continued, "So the first test we took had a sample of-."

"Can we just cut to the chase?" Carl asked. "Please," he pleaded.

"Okay," said the doctor looking at him kindly. "To cut to the chase, Carl, you have some sperm, not a lot, but some sperm with great motility," Doctor Farber said slowly. He paused. "You look puzzled Carl," Dr. Farber said.

"What?" asked Carl.

"Carl, do you know what this means?" Matt said excitedly shaking his brother's arm.

"What?" asked Carl the shock clearly displaying on his face.

"There is a possibility that you could be a father," said

the doctor, "Actually, a really good possibility."

"Holy shit, holy shit, holy shit!" yelled Carl jumping up and walking in circles in the office, the tears filling his eyes and streaming down his face. "Oh my god, oh my god, thank you, thank you," Carl said going to the doctor. "Thank you," he said shaking his hand.

"Congratulations Carl," Dr. Farber said smiling.

Matt turned and grabbed his brother and hugged him. "Oh my god, oh my god," he said to his brother sobbing in his arms.

***

Carl could hardly sit still in the car on the ride to Rena's apartment. "Are you sure you know where it is?" Carl asked Matt for the fourth time.

"Yes, Carl, relax, I dropped her off before, remember that? We'll be there soon, *calm down* buddy," Matt said patting his brother's arm.

"I have to tell Rena, I have to tell her, oh man, com'on, I have to tell her," Carl said looking anxiously out of the car. "Should I just get out and run?" he turned and asked Matt.

"No, Carl, relax, we are almost there," Matt said starting to sound annoyed.

"I know, okay sorry," said Carl sitting back.

He needed to see Rena desperately, needed to tell her he loved her and that they were going to have a family. "Not that she didn't know that," he thought. She had had faith from the start that the baby was his. And god, he loved her even more for it. He had accused her of cheating, what a jerk he had been. He needed to see her now, to clear things between them.

Matt turned into the apartment complex and parked in visitors parking. Carl ran out of the car into the building and waited for Matt outside the elevator.

"What floor?" he asked pressing the up button continuously.

"That doesn't make it come any faster," Matt said grinning at him.

The elevator opened and Carl jumped in. Matt followed and pressed the fourth floor. "Fourth floor?" Carl asked. "I could have run up the stairs!" he said excitedly.

Matt laughed. "It's great to see you this way Carl," he said.

The elevator door opened and Carl dashed out. He looked both ways down the hall then looked at Matt. "Which way?" he asked.

"This way," said Matt grinning and walking up to Rena's door.

Carl knocked on the door to Rena's apartment. No answer. He knocked again and could hear someone say, "Coming." "Com'on, com'on," he said quietly under his breath, having trouble standing still. The door opened and a tall, lanky red haired girl answered the door.

"Is Rena here?" asked Carl looking past the girl.

"Who?" asked the girl.

"Rena, she lives here," said Matt.

"Oh," said the girl smiling, the realization showing on her face. "No, she's not here," she said smiling.

"Well where is she?" asked Carl.

"I'm not sure," said the girl, "I'm subletting from her for a couple of months."

"What?" asked Carl incredulously. He looked at Matt. "What the fuck?" he asked his brother.

"Carl," said Matt sternly and then glanced at the girl. "Do you have any idea where she went?" he asked the girl. "It is really important that we get hold of her," he said.

"Well she did give me a number where to reach her," the girl said, "But I'm not sure if I should be just handing it out."

"You are not serious," said Carl glaring at the girl.

"Carl, seriously," said Matt. "You're not helping," he said sternly to his younger brother. "Look," he said to the girl calmly. "Carl, my brother just found out some great news, and he is the father of Rena's baby, so we really need to get a hold of her," he said. The girl looked apprehensive. "She was here with another woman, Anna," he said.

"Oh yes," the girl smiled.

"We are friends with Anna," he said.

"Well," said the girl, "I heard them say they were going to stay at a friend's place for a bit." "That's all I can say," she said starting to close the door.

"Okay" sighed Matt. "Thank you," he said thanking the girl.

"Anna's friend," he said to Carl who was pacing the floor.

"Anna's friend? She's at a friend of Anna's?" Carl asked confounded. "Anna has a zillion friends," he said in disbelief. *Crap. She was gone.*

CHAPTER 39

Rena looked out over the deck at the forest. They had arrived two days earlier in Aurora and Rena was feeling at home already. The house was spacious and modern and Rena felt like she was at a resort. The backyard overlooked a forested area and had a beautiful deck with lounge chairs and a barbeque. Anna's friend was away overseas so Anna had asked if they could stay at her place.

"Not that there is anything wrong with this apartment," Anna had said looking a little sheepish. "But once Simon gets here, this place will be a little too small," she said glancing around Rena's place.

Rena laughed. Anna liked the finer things in life, and Rena's apartment was 1000 square feet, and in an older building that needed renovations. She grinned at her friend. "It's okay Anna, I love you anyway, even though you hate my apartment," she said laughing. Anna looked alarmed.

"No, Rena, really, I don't," she said glancing at her friend then grinning sheepishly. "Am I that bad?" she asked.

Rena got up from the couch and walked over to her friend. "Yes, you are spoiled rotten Anna, and that is why I love you," she said hugging her friend. "Let's get out of here...your friends place sounds amazing!"

So here they were. Forty-five minute drive North of Toronto in a million dollar home overlooking a small forest. Rena lay back on the lounge chair and took a deep breath. She rubbed her belly. She was starting to show. She looked down and smiled at the change in her body. She wished Carl had been here to see it. He would have laid his hand on her belly and kissed it. She knew he would have. She sighed. "If only he had believed me," she thought. She rested further back on the lounge chair and closed her eyes. She couldn't think about him anymore, it hurt too much.

***

Carl paced back and forth in Falcone's kitchen. "Where can she be Falcone?" he asked wringing his hands through his hair.

"I don't know man, you know my cousin," said Falcone, searching on his phone.

"Calm down Carl, this isn't helping," said Matt at the sidelines. They had left Rena's apartment and had driven straight to Falcone to see if he knew anything. But he hadn't.

Since they had got to Falcone's place, Falcone had called at least a dozen of Anna and Simon's friends but nobody knew where Anna was, and some didn't even know she was in the country. Falcone was faced with making excuses and explanations for Anna neglecting to let them know she was in Toronto, and then hurriedly trying to get off the phone so he could call the next number he could find. Falcone sighed. "I need a beer," he said getting up from the table and walking to the fridge.

"Let me call," said Carl.

"Sure," said Falcone, "Start at 'S', I think she knows everyone under there" he said talking from within the open door of the fridge.

Carl looked at the list. There were at least six names under 'S'. Susan, Samantha, Shar, Sadie. "Are you sure these are Anna's friends?" Carl asked.

"Yah, yah" nodded Falcone handing a beer to Matt and opening his to take a swig.

"I don't want to end up calling one of your conquests y'know," Carl said.

"That I cannot guarantee," said Falcone laughing.

Matt's phone rang and he left to take the call in another other room. Carl tried four numbers to no avail. Either the callers were out, or no answering machine picked up. "This is frustrating," said Carl.

"Has she still not answered your texts?" he asked Falcone.

"No," said Falcone checking his phone. "She either is somewhere with no service or busy shopping and not answering it. You know my cousin," he said. "Have a beer buddy," Falcone said sliding a bottle down the counter to Carl.

"No man, I need to keep a clear head," said Carl. He needed to find her. The longer he didn't see her or talk to her, the longer he worried that she could have changed her mind about him. He couldn't afford to have that happen.

Matt walked back into the kitchen. "I have to go Carl," he said to his brother. "The girls have something going on and Martha can't drive them," he said.

"It's okay Matt," Carl said standing up and hugging his brother. "Thanks for all of your help today, I appreciate it."

Matt patted him on the back. "Hang in there kiddo, it will be okay," he said.

"I hope so," said Carl.

"You both love each other, that doesn't fade, don't worry," he said reassuringly.

"I hope you're right," Carl said.

"What letter are we on now?" asked Falcone.

"Still have two on 'S'," said Carl.

"Let me do it," said Falcone taking the phone.

Carl left the room and walked to the back yard. He needed some fresh air. It had been a long day and an emotional one. He sat down on one of the deck chairs. Falcone came out from the kitchen chatting on the phone. Carl sat up.

"So you're not sure where she went, right?" Falcone asked the person on the line. "Okay, right, sure thanks," he said looking at Carl and gesturing madly. "There's a call coming in," he said to Carl hanging up on the other line. "Where the fuck *have* you been?" Carl could hear Falcone say on the line.

***

233

The deep brown eyes bore into her skull. They haunted her. They wouldn't leave her alone. They were calling out to her. They were the only eyes she had ever felt she could dive into. They were deep, full, and endless. They kept calling her into their depths. She wanted to go there. "Rena, Rena," they called.

"Rena, Rena," the voice called to her. "Rena wake up," the voice said.

"Leave me alone," she thought half-awake. She didn't want to wake up from this dream.

"Rena, please," the voice said again.

Rena forced her eyes to open. The sun was shining and she squinted against the glare seeing a shadow of a form.

"Rena it's me," the voice said.

The shadow moved closer. Rena looked up at the brownest eyes she had ever seen.

"Rena," the eyes smiled at her.

Rena bolted upright. "Carl?" she said still groggy.

"Yes, it's me," Carl said kneeling down beside the lounge chair.

"What are you doing here?" asked Rena waking up quickly.

"Rena, we have to talk," Carl said.

"I can't do this now," Rena thought. She looked at him thinking of the turmoil she had been through the past few weeks. "Carl, you keep saying that, that we need to talk, and I keep saying the same thing, get tested!" Rena said jumping up from the chair and pushing past him frustrated.

"Rena, wait!" Carl said grabbing her arm before she could reach the door to go inside. "Rena, I did get tested." "I got tested," he repeated looking at her earnestly.

"Oh," said Rena stunned. "So he finally did it; took long enough," Rena thought.

"Rena, the baby is mine, Rena it's mine!" Carl said smiling at her.

"I already knew that," Rena snapped.

Carl's smile faded. "I know, I shouldn't have said it like that," Carl said dejectedly. "Rena, look, I'm sorry. I'm sorry I didn't believe you," Carl said pausing. It's just that, it seemed impossible that I could ever be a father, and I couldn't fathom how it could be true."

"You didn't believe me," Rena said her eyes filling with tears.

"I know Rena, I know. I was a jerk, I'm so sorry," Carl said his eyes watering, "but I never stopped loving you, you have to believe that."

"But," Rena interrupted tears streaming down her face, "You didn't believe me, you didn't *trust* me. You looked at me like I was someone you didn't know, like I was a piece of dirt, something you could throw away," she sobbed.

"Rena, don't, I never...," Carl stepped forward tears now welling in his eyes.

"No," said Rena backing away. "Y-you can't just come here and think everything will be okay. "You *can't*," she sobbed.

"Oh my god, Rena please," Carl pleaded wiping away his tears with his hands. "Please Rena, listen to me, please," he begged.

"No, no, just leave me alone," Rena said turning and running into the house.

***

Carl sat down on the lounge chair where Rena had been. He knew he had hurt her. He knew he had pushed her away. She had every right to be angry with him. He wrung his hands through his hair. He desperately needed her to forgive him, to give him another chance. "Damn," he thought. He had let his past get in the way of his future, and it was destroying him. It was destroying his chance at happiness with Rena. He sighed. He sure knew how to screw things up. Falcone came out of the house onto the deck.

"That was explosive," he said trying to make light.

"Yah," said Carl, "Not what I was hoping for at all, but she has a right to be upset," he said looking up at his friend.

"Yah, she does," said Falcone, "But it doesn't take away from the fact that she is pregnant with your kid," he said defensively.

"She might need more time," Carl said the realization hitting him.

"Are you serious?" Falcone asked sarcastically sitting down on the lounge next to Carl. "You and Rena have had tons of space. After all this, getting tested and searching for her, you're going to give up?" he asked sounding frustrated with his friend.

"Not give up, just give her time and space," Carl said.

"I thought that's what you *were* doing," said Falcone.

"No, I was just being an ass."

***

Rena walked through the woods. The entrance was located at the end of the street and Rena had walked there quickly. The trees were green and lush in the forest and Rena inhaled the fresh air. She needed to relax. She didn't want to cause any stress for the baby. She hadn't expected to see Carl. Sure, she knew maybe one day he would show up, but she hadn't expected it to be so soon. She had just got used to the fact that she might have to bring up her baby alone with Anna, when Carl popped back into the picture all excited that he was the father. "Jackass," thought Rena. He had basically accused her of being a slut, and a liar, and now he was trying to win her back. But Rena wasn't sure, if he was back for *her*, or if it was just for the baby.

She sat down on a tree stump. A cool breeze brushed her face and it felt comforting and soothing. She loved nature. It always brought her back to herself. She had fallen hard for Carl. It had been romantic and he had made her feel like the most beautiful woman on earth. She had felt loved, loveable and loving, things she had never felt with Jarod. With Carl at her side, she had started to believe she could do anything. And then he had pushed her away. He had wanted to talk to her, but did not want to listen. He told her how he thought she felt, and how he thought things were, instead of letting her tell him how she really felt and how things really were. She sighed. She knew he had had a difficult past, that he was as scared as her to be hurt again. She exhaled slowly. It did explain his reaction, his disbelief when she had told him. He must have been shocked. Actually, she knew he had been; it had been written all over his face. But now he was back and she could tell he was excited. He hadn't expected to be a father. "This must be a like a miracle for him," Rena thought. But sadly, it didn't change anything. She couldn't be with him if he was just with her for the baby. He had pushed her aside so easily once, what would stop him from doing that again? She couldn't let him do that to a child. She wiped away a loan tear that rolled down her cheek. She sighed again and blew out a slow breath, getting up from the stump. She would walk for a little while longer; she needed to think.

CHAPTER 40

Carl got up from this brother's couch and answered the phone. After he had talked with Falcone, he had left Anna's friends place to think. He had told Anna to let Rena know that he had gone, but that she could give him a call when she was ready. He answered the phone anticipating that it was Rena. "Thank God," he thought, "Thank God." But it was not Rena. Anna's frantic voice greeted him.

"Carl, it's Anna is Rena with you?" she asked sounding worried.

"No, I haven't seen her, what's going on Anna?" he asked getting a sinking feeling in his stomach.

"I haven't seen her since you left," Anna said. "I know she went to the woods for a walk, but it's going to get dark soon and I haven't heard from her," Anna said.

Carl felt the panic rise in his chest. "Did you try and call her cell?" he asked. "Of course she did," he thought.

"Yes, of course," said Anna echoing his thoughts. "Carl,

239

I'm getting worried," she said.

"Sit tight, I'll be there as fast as I can," Carl said hanging up the phone.

Carl arrived at Anna's friend's place twenty-five minutes later with Falcone pulling into the driveway behind him. The twenty-five minutes had felt like a lifetime and he had dialed Rena's phone repeatedly on the drive, but she had not answered. He ran out of the car up to the front door where Anna was standing.

"Should we go into the woods to find her?" Anna asked.

Falcone rushed up to the door. "Yah, it's getting dark, we have to find her if that is where she is," he said determinedly.

"Of course that's where she is," Anna retorted angrily.

"Anna, she could have gone somewhere else to be alone," Falcone said, exasperated with his cousin.

"She wouldn't do that without telling me," Anna said defiantly.

"Okay, Okay, guys," said Carl, "we are wasting time." "How many entrances are there to the woods?" he asked Anna.

"I don't know, I think two or three, could be more," Anna said.

"Where's the closest one?" Carl asked her.

"Down at the cul de sac, at the end of the road," Anna pointed.

"Okay, you wait here, Falc, let's get our flashlights and flares and go find her," Carl ordered.

"On it," said Falcone rushing to his car to grab a flashlight and headlamp. "I have my bike headlamp," he said tossing it to Carl, "that will help."

Carl grabbed the headlamp, put it on, and then grabbed a flashlight and a couple of flares from his car. "Okay, let's go," he said starting to run down the driveway. "Anna be by the phone," he ordered turning around.

"Please find her," Anna pleaded as the men ran to the entrance of the woods.

They arrived at the entrance in less than a minute and started following the path. Carl called out to Rena but heard nothing. They continued to walk down the trail and got to a fork in the path. "Let's split up," said Falcone. "I'll take this way, you go the other way," he suggested.

"Okay," said Carl, "Keep your phone on."

Carl walked down the path calling out to Rena. He stopped a few times thinking he had heard something but realized he could hear Falcone calling in the distance. The dusk that was there when they had arrived, was starting to turn to darkness and Carl was worried that they soon would not be able to see off the trails.

He kept walking and called out to Rena, passing a small clearing in a wooded area near a small river. "If I hadn't been looking for her, it would be a nice place to kiss her," thought Carl. He shook his head. He didn't have time to daydream. He had to find her. He kept walking down the trail peering into the woods and calling out to Rena. Twenty minutes later, he met Falcone coming from the other way.

"No sign of her?" he asked his friend.

"Nothing, and it's getting darker," said Falcone. "We

might need to get more help."

Carl felt sick. It was getting dark and Rena was alone and probably scared somewhere in the woods. He didn't want to think of what could have happened to her. He should have been gentler when he spoke to her this afternoon, should have considered her feelings. But no, he had been excited and pig-headed, only thinking of himself. "Falcone," he looked at his friend, desperation starting to envelop him.

"We'll find her," said Falcone confidently. "You loop back round, then we'll meet up again. If we don't find her we'll call it in," said Falcone taking charge.

"Okay," said Carl, relieved that his friend took over. He couldn't think straight anymore.

Carl walked back down the trail he had come from. The darkness had fallen quickly and Carl turned on the headlamp so he could see. The light was dim. "Damn Falcone," he thought, "You need to charge the battery." He called out for Rena. Silence. He walked a bit longer and called out again. Nothing. He kept walking and got to the wooded clearing again. He was about to pass by it, but was drawn to the area. It was a great kissing spot. "What the heck is wrong with me?" he thought. He walked closer to the clearing. He could imagine his hands in her hair, her head tilted back as he kissed her mouth and her glorious neck. *What was wrong with him? Was he insane? How could he be thinking of this when he couldn't find her?* But he felt her here. He stopped. He *felt* her.

"Rena," Carl called out starting to move around the clearing calling her name. "Rena," he called, thinking how frantic he sounded. He could feel her presence, it like she was here. "Rena." He walked toward the river and could make out a log right beside the water's edge. "Rena would have liked to sit on that," he thought moving closer. He froze. He heard something. "Rena?" he called taking a step forward. He heard it again. A moan. "Rena, Rena, where are you?" he called out moving the headlamp around toward the sound. The dim light caught the stump as Carl moved his head. "What the," Carl said moving the lamp to focus on the stump. It was Rena! He rushed over to her. He could see under the headlamp that she was on her side. Her crumpled body lay still. He called her name, lifted her head, and noticed the blood on his hands. "Rena," he said calling her name. Rena moaned. Carl quickly ripped off his shirt, wrapped it around her head, and applied pressure. With his other hand, he used the speed dial on his phone and called Falcone. "I found her, we need an ambulance," he said frantically.

"Light a flare, so I can find you," Falcone said.

Carl wrapped his shirt a bit tighter around Rena's head and then took out the flare and lit it. The flare lit up the sky.

"Okay, I see where you are, save the other one buddy for when the ambulance comes. I will call Anna," Falcone said. "What else do you need?" Falcone asked.

"Not sure, she is bleeding from her head and isn't very responsive," said Carl. "Falcone, if anything happens to her."

"Don't think like that," Falcone interrupted. "She will be okay, let me call Anna," he said disconnecting the line.

It felt like ages, but finally the ambulance attendants arrived. Falcone, Anna, and Matt followed them into the clearing. "It looks like she fell and hit her head," Carl said to the attendants and his friends.

Anna rushed to Carl and hugged him. The attendants

reached Rena's side and called out to her but only got moans in response. They quickly tended to Rena's head wound and carefully got her onto a stretcher and started moving her down the trail. The rest of them followed.

"Oh Carl," said Anna clinging to his arm.

"Anna!" Falcone said pulling Anna away from Carl. "Leave him, he has enough," Falcone said hugging his cousin.

Carl's eyes and feet followed the stretcher like his life depended on it. And it did. Without Rena, his world had no meaning. She had come into his life quickly, and seemed to have gone just as quickly. What they had was intense, powerful, and amazing. He couldn't live without her. She had to be okay. His life depended on it.

CHAPTER 41

Rena woke up with a terrific headache. She could hear noises and tried to open her eyes, but the light was too bright. "Ow," she thought feeling a sharp jab of pain bolt between her eyes. She tried to focus in her mind. *Where was she?* The noises around her sounded unfamiliar and she could hear voices, but she couldn't make out the words. "Ow," she inwardly cursed again as she tried to open her eyes.

"Rena," a strange voice called her name.

She tried again to open her eyes. Ow! The light bore into her forehead like a laser.

"Rena, wake up," the voice said.

Rena tried again to open her eyes. She could see a foggy image of someone looming above her. "Ow," she said aloud as a light shone in her eyes.

"I know it hurts Rena," the voice said. "Try to open your eyes again, you can do it Rena," the voice said reassuringly.

Rena blinked and opened her eyes again.

"Hello there," the man said, his image starting to come into Rena's focus. "I'm Doctor Derricks, Rena. You're in the hospital; you had a fall. You're going to be okay, but I need to check you out, okay?"

"Ow," Rena said again blinking. It hurt when she blinked.

"Yes, it hurts, that's okay, it will get better," the doctor said starting to feel around her head. "Rena, I'm going to put the head of the bed up a bit so I can look at the back of your head," he said.

"Okay," Rena croaked out. Her voice sounded hoarse and foreign to her. She felt the bed move up and heard a woman's voice beside her.

"You okay Rena?" Rena turned her head to see a nurse beside her.

"Ow, my head," she said as the bed moved up.

"Yes, I know it hurts," the nurse said, "all done now."

"Okay Rena, just going to feel the back of your head," the doctor said. She felt him lift her head and move his hands around the back near her neck. He moved up further.

"Ow!" Rena said as he touched her.

"Yes, you have a big goose egg back here," he said. "You can lie back on the pillow now," the doctor said.

She saw him and the nurse move to the end of the bed and could hear them murmur. The doctor turned back to look at her. "I'll be back to check on you again, Rena. We need to get an ultrasound done to see how the baby is doing," he said.

The words smacked Rena back into reality like a bucket of ice water. "Oh my god, my baby, is it okay?" Rena asked feeling frantic. The nurse moved back to her side.

"Yes, love, we have a monitor on you, see?" she said as she pointed to Rena's stomach that was strapped with something like looked like a belt. "The heartbeat is strong but we just want to have a look to be sure," she said.

"Okay," said Rena feeling a bit relieved. Her head was starting to throb. "My head hurts," she told the nurse.

"Yes, I will give you something for the pain," the nurse head.

"Will it hurt my baby?" Rena asked starting to feel frightened.

"No, it won't," said the nurse kindly. "You are in good hands, we'll take good care of you and your baby," the nurse said. "Now Rena, I want you to do something for me," the nurse continued.

"What?" asked Rena tiredly.

"I want you to try and stay awake," the nurse said. "You had a good knock on your head and it is important that you stay awake."

"Oh," said Rena not liking it at all. "But I feel tired and my head is so sore."

"The medication will help, but staying awake is important Rena," the nurse said.

She handed Rena a small cup with pills and helped Rena sit up as she took them with a sip of water. Her hands were shaky and she felt chilled. "I feel cold," Rena said.

"Let me get you a warm blanket," the nurse said.

She left through the curtains and came back two minutes later. She laid the blanket on Rena. "Ooh, that is so warm," said Rena feeling the warmth of the blanket covering her body.

"Yes, it's a warming blanket, it will help," the nurse said smiling at her kindly. "Your friend Anna would like to come in and see you," the nurse said.

"Oh yes, please," said Rena tears filling her eyes.

"Okay love," the nurse said patting her hand and leaving the room.

Anna came through the curtains a minute later. "Rena," she cried running to Rena's bed and giving her a hug. Rena held on to her friend and sobbed. The sobbing hurt her head but she couldn't stop.

"Ow," said Rena feeling Anna react and pull back. "No," said Rena grabbing her friend. "I need you Anna," she said sobbing.

Anna held her and both of them cried. "Rena, we were so worried," Anna said once they had calmed down. She moved from the bed to grab a box of Kleenex and passed some to Rena. Rena wiped her eyes and blew her nose.

"Ugh," she said wincing at the pain it caused. "Everything hurts," she said starting to feel the soreness in her arms, hands and legs as well as her head.

"What happened, Rena?" Anna asked wiping her tears

from her face. She went to sit beside Rena and grabbed her hand.

"I-I'm not sure," said Rena still feeling a little shaky. "What happened?" asked Rena.

"We found you in the forest Rena. You fell, or it looks like you did," she said.

"Oh," said Rena still trying to remember. Her head was still pounding but a little less than before.

"It got dark and we were worried," Anna said.

Rena was puzzled. Why couldn't she remember anything? "Ow," she said moving on the bed.

"Rena, are you okay?" asked Anna.

"Just achy," Rena replied. "Do you know what happened to me Anna?" she asked her friend again.

"Rena, maybe you need some rest," Anna replied.

"I'm not allowed to sleep," Rena said wanly.

"I know," Anna said, "I just meant that you might want to take a break from trying to remember," she replied smiling at her friend.

"I know," Rena sighed.

"You might remember that way," Anna suggested.

"Maybe," said Rena not feeling convinced. She sighed. She was a little worried that she could not remember what had happened. "Anna can we go over it?" she asked her friend again.

"Are you sure Rena? I don't want to push you," Anna

said looking worried.

"Yes, I am sure, I am feeling better," Rena said trying to sit up more and smile at her friend.

"Hmmm," Anna said.

"Hmmm? Anna, I am fine, really Anna!" said Rena exasperated.

"Okay okay," Anna said relenting, "But if it's too much you will let me know, right?"

"Of course," Rena said convincingly inwardly crossing her fingers.

Anna looked straight at her. "Rena, you remember you are pregnant, right?" she asked earnestly.

"I'm *pregnant*?" Rena responded trying her best to look and sound shocked. The pain medication was starting to kick in and the throbbing in her head had subsided to a dull ache. The look on Anna's face made her break out in laughter. "Ow, ow, it hurts, oh Anna, of course I know I'm pregnant," she howled.

"Rena, that wasn't funny," Anna said sounding annoyed and trying not to smile.

"I know, sorry," said Rena sheepishly. "That laughing hurt," she said holding her head wincing.

"Geeze Rena, take it easy," Anna said admonishing her friend.

"I know, ow," Rena said moving in the bed.

She held her stomach. "Rena?" Anna looked at her questioningly.

"Just feels a bit odd, that's all," Rena said leaning back on her pillow. She took a deep breath and breathed out slowly.

"Do you want me to call the nurse?" Anna asked.

"No, Anna, it's okay," Rena said wriggling again. "Okay, so tell me what happened to me," Rena said changing the subject.

Anna took a slow breath. "Okay, just relax though, okay?"

"Okay," Rena said nodding.

"So you went out for a walk in the woods. You remember telling me that right?"

"I think so," said Rena trying to rack her brain.

"You had just been talking with Carl," Anna said softly.

Carl. The recollection hit her like a brick wall. Rena felt like she couldn't breathe. She felt a lump in her throat.

"Rena?" Anna asked looking anxiously at her friend.

"Oh Anna," Rena cried the tears starting to fall down her face.

"Rena, you are supposed to be resting," Anna said grabbing her hand. "Just relax, don't think about this," she said.

"H-how c-can't I?" Rena asked shakily. The pain in her head was starting to throb again. Anna handed her a tissue and Rena wiped her face. "H-he only cares about the baby," Rena said the tears continuing to flow. "I-I thought he l-loved me, but," she said stopping mid-sentence as she felt a twinge in her stomach. "Oh, Anna, I

251

can't lose this baby," Rena cried. "It's all I have, Anna."

"Rena, what's wrong?" Anna asked.

"Ooh," Rena gasped grabbing her stomach.

Anna quickly ran out to the hallway and called the nurse. The nurse came scurrying the room with Anna in close pursuit. "I thought I told you to relax, sweetie," she told Rena checking her IV and wiping her tears. "Where does it hurt love?" she asked putting her hand on Rena's stomach.

"My h-head, my stomach," Rena stuttered.

"Okay let me check," the nurse said connecting the monitor on Rena's stomach. "Okay relax, sweetie, let me see if we can find your baby," she said moving the monitor around. "Relax sweetie," she said again.

Rena took a deep breath. "I have to relax," she thought. *This baby is all I have left.* She heard the sound before the nurse told her. "Oh, is that the baby?" she said hearing the beating and swooshing sound.

"Yes, strong heartbeat," the nurse said reassuringly. "Now, your friend must go, so we can prepare you for the ultrasound," she said.

"Can't she stay?" Rena asked anxiously. Rena thought the nurse looked surprised.

"Sure," she said, "Be right back."

Anna went by Rena's side. "Rena," she said, "You want me to call Carl?" she asked gently.

"He only cares about the baby, not *me*," Rena said.

"No, Ren," Anna said interrupted by the nurse coming

back into the room.

"We'll go in about half an hour," the nurse said, "Hang tight."

Once the nurse left the room, Anna turned to Rena again. "Rena, Carl is the one who found you in the woods. He was so worried about you."

"No he wasn't," said Rena, he only cares about the baby," she said adamantly.

"That's not true Rena," Anna said firmly. "When he found out you were missing I have never seen anyone's face turn the shade of white his did. He was really scared. For *you*. He went crazy getting everyone out to search and he would have searched forever Rena."

"I-I was missing?" Rena said floored.

"Yes, you must have fallen near a river and hit your head. Carl found you Rena, and he was frantic. He looked really scared for you," she said passionately.

"B-but he accused me of cheating on him," Rena said the tears starting to flow again.

"Yes, he did, and that is something you have to talk with him about. But he does love you Rena."

"He only came back because he found out the baby was his," Rena said wiping her tears. Anna went to get the box of Kleenex and handed one to Rena.

"Rena, he told Falcone he was going to stick by you no matter what. He loves you that much Rena."

"But," Rena sighed.

"I know Rena, but you have to understand why he

reacted why he did. He was scared. And maybe that's why you reacted how you did too. You were scared," Anna said gently.

"What are you talking about?" asked Rena turning to look at her friend.

"You told him to leave you alone Rena." "I did *what?*" Rena asked stunned.

"Yes," said Anna.

Rena tried to remember what she had said, but she could remember nothing. "But he went to find me anyway?"

"Of course," Anna said consolingly stroking Rena's hair. "He loves you, Rena. Sure, I am sure he loves this baby too, but he loves you. And he knows he upset you."

"Is he here?" Rena asked.

CHAPTER 42

Carl sat in the coffee shop holding a mug between his hands. He couldn't let the mug go. His hands were shaking and the mug gave him something to hold on to. He had left the hospital once he had known that she was okay. He wanted to stay, badly, but he didn't want to upset Rena any more than he already had. She asked for him to leave her alone, and he had to honour that. God knows, he had made enough accusations to dishonour her. He needed to respect her wishes, even though it was killing him inside. The doctor had come out and told him that Rena was fine, but would need to be observed as she had a concussion. The baby was fine too, but Carl had barely heard that. The minute he knew Rena was fine he collapsed in the waiting room seat and held his head in his hands. He loved her so much that it hurt inside. He needed her to be okay, to be happy. He would do anything for that, even if it meant not being by her side.

His phone rang in his jacket pocket and Carl shakenly put the mug down. He could see the stares of some of the patrons in the restaurant. He looked a right mess, and he knew it. But this had been the longest day of his life. He got the phone out of his pocket and looked at it. It was Falcone. He had asked Falcone to stay at the hospital and let him know how Rena was doing. Even if he couldn't be there, he had to know she was doing okay. "Falc," he said hoarsely into the phone. "My voice doesn't sound like my own," he thought.

"Carl, you better get here now," said Falcone, "Rena...."

Carl didn't wait to hear the rest. He dropped money on the table and took off.

He arrived on the hospital floor and could feel his heart pounding. He had run all the way from the coffee shop. He was in no shape to drive. It had taken him fifteen minutes at a full out sprint, and he was panting. "Falc, where is she?" Carl asked his heart beating a mile a minute seeing Falcone in the waiting room at the end of the hall.

"She's," Falcone pointed towards the door where Rena was. "Carl calm down, she's okay," he called after Carl who went rushing into the room in the direction Falcone was pointing.

Carl got into the room and stopped. She was on the bed lying on her back. He could see the baby bump that was pushing out from her stomach. Her head was bandaged and he could see an IV in her arm. A nurse was by her side working with something.

"R," he tried to get her name out but he couldn't speak.

She turned to look at him and gave him a tiny smile. "My god, she is beautiful," he thought. "R-rena," he said approaching her. He grabbed her hand, kissed it, and held it to his mouth. His whole body was shaking.

"Carl, are you okay?" she asked him. He held her hand, and started to cry.

256

"I'm okay, Carl," Rena said, "They are going to do an ultrasound. Can you hear me? We are going to see our baby," Rena said.

He could feel her other hand stroke his head. He looked up. She was looking at him, tears running down her face onto her pretty nose and cheeks. Carl gasped for air. He couldn't get the words out. He needed her to hear them.

"Rena," he croaked. "I'm so sorry," he said kissing her hands.

"M-me too," said Rena leaning forward to kiss his hands that were clasping hers. "Ow," she said as her head cried out in defiance.

"Okay," said the nurse, "Let's calm down and have a look at this beautiful life you both created, yes?" she said looking at the two of them and handing them a box of tissue. She pulled a chair up for Carl. "Sit down daddy, you look like you need it," she said kindly.

Carl moved the chair beside Rena's bed and grabbed her hand. "I'm not going to let go," he thought.

"This might feel a bit cold," the technician said pouring a gel-like substance on Rena's belly.

"Ooh, that is cold," Rena said.

"It will warm up," the technician said turning the monitor so they both could see it. "Let's have a look at your baby," she said.

Carl moved Rena's hands towards him and kissed them. "I love *you* Rena," he said.

"I know," she said tears streaming down her face as she saw the image of her baby for the first time.

***

Carl woke up feeling energetic. Rena was getting out of the hospital today and Carl was picking her up. He had wanted to stay at the hospital the night before, but was shooed out by the nurse and told to come back in the morning. He couldn't blame her. He was a right mess last night and probably looked and smelled something awful. But he was on a high. After seeing Rena was okay, and that she had forgiven him and still loved him, he felt his life could not get any better. And then seeing his baby; that had been the ultimate experience. He had got home late and showered, and it had taken hours to fall asleep. But somehow, he felt like he had slept for hours. He still couldn't believe that he had fathered a child. It seemed like a miracle. Heck, it was a miracle! *What did I do to deserve this?* He had said that to himself many times over the years, but in a very different context. His life since he had met Rena had just been one miracle after another. It was surreal, and he did not want it to end. Ever.

He quickly got up and checked his phone. He still had time to go for a run and have a shower before he got Rena. He felt more alive than he had in weeks. Rena had that effect on him. She made him see the same world differently, like he was being introduced to it all over again. He quickly got dressed in his running gear and headed out the door. The air felt fresh, clean and crisp. He could hear the birds chirping their morning songs and hear his footsteps on the pavement. Life was grand.

CHAPTER 43

*I love **you**, Rena. I love **you**, Rena. I love **you**.*

Rena woke up in her hospital bed feeling groggy. Her head still hurt but nothing like the pain she had felt the day before. She felt a fluttering movement in her belly and smiled. "It is probably just gas," she thought, but it felt special to think it might be her baby. She took a deep breath in and slowly let it out. She felt relaxed, even though she was tired. The nurses had woken her up every hour or so during the night and each time they did, Rena had felt a twinge of pain when she moved her head. But at some point during the night, they had stopped waking her, and Rena had slept soundly. Carl was supposed to come and get her today. Rena felt the excitement build up in her. She had missed him. She felt the fluttering again. "Did you miss him too?" she asked caressing her belly.

"Is your baby moving?" a pleasant voice asked. Rena looked up to see the smiling face of her morning nurse.

"I'm not sure," she said grinning. "I feel a fluttery feeling, but it might be gas," she said sheepishly.

The nurse smiled. "Babies feel like butterflies," she said and came and put her hand on Rena's belly. The fluttering started again.

"Oh," said Rena. "I felt it again."

"It's your little butterfly," the nurse said smiling.

"A butterfly," thought Rena. Butterflies were free, beautiful, and delicate. When Jarod had died, Rena had felt like a butterfly waiting to emerge from its cocoon. She knew she was free, she just didn't know how to be. Carl had shown her how to free herself from the confines of her cocoon. He had helped her to recognize her own beauty, her own ability to love and be loved, and her own freedom. He had jumped in headfirst even though he had been afraid himself. He had helped her find the inner strength and power she didn't know she had. Her belly fluttered again. "Thank you, thank you, and thank you," Rena whispered under her breath.

Two hours later Rena sat beside Carl in his car. It had taken awhile to get out the hospital with the last minute check by the doctor, paperwork, medication and instructions. Carl had listened attentively to everything that he was told and had assured the doctors, nurses and staff that Rena would be in good hands. His attentiveness was charming and Rena noticed all of the nurses giving her encouraging smiles. "They are loving him as much as I do," Rena thought grinning to herself. Carl had carefully helped Rena into the wheelchair and had helped her into his car.

"Nice car," Rena had said when she saw the blue Camaro.

"Summer car," Carl had said grinning.

"What's the winter car?" Rena had asked.

"You don't want to know about that one," Carl said grinning.

"Will it fit a car seat?" Rena asked innocently.

"No child of mine will be in that car," Carl said.

"You mean we are going car shopping?" Rena asked delightedly.

"Looks like it sweetheart," Carl said leaning over and giving her a kiss. "But first things first, let's get you home," he said.

"Home?" Rena asked.

"Yes, my home Rena," Carl said seriously. "I promised Anna I would bring you back to her since I am working nights this week, but first I want you to *myself*," he said with promise in his eyes.

Rena felt a flash of heat in her body. "I thought the doctor said I had to take it easy," she said teasing.

"Oh *you* will take it easy," Carl said, "I will handle *everything*," he said smiling confidently.

"All of the *details*?" Rena asked grinning.

"I will handle *every* detail," Carl said with meaning.

"I bet you will," murmured Rena smiling and feeling the warmth between her legs.

***

She got what he promised. They had got to Carl's home and Rena had barely time to notice what it looked like. "You can explore later, after *I have*," Carl growled seductively, scooped her up quickly, and brought her up the stairs and into his room. His furniture was dark but the room colours were rich and warm and Rena liked it.

"Oh, I like this room," Rena said looking around as Carl laid her on the bed. She turned to looked at his nightstand and noticed it was full of books. She leaned closer. "The Expectant Father," "A Practical Handbook for New Dads, Partner," "A complete guide to childbirth for dads," she read aloud. She turned to look at Carl. "Carl," was all that came out.

Carl looked into Rena eyes and caressed her mouth with his fingers. "I want to be a good dad to our baby Rena," he said tears shining his eyes.

"You already are," Rena said touching his cheek.

He leaned forward and as his lips touched hers, Rena felt like she was on fire. She could feel the heat rise through her body until her whole body tingled with anticipation. His tongue delved into her mouth and met hers, touching caressing, moving, and exploring. He moved closer to her on the bed and pulled her to him. She could feel the heat emanating from his body and could feel his erection getting bigger as he pressed against her groin. She moaned.

"Rena," he said breathlessly looking into her eyes.

"Kiss me," she said pulling him back down to her.

Carl plunged his tongue back into her mouth, this time, teasing, sucking and gently biting her lip. Rena felt the moist wetness between her legs. She could feel her nipples straining against her bra as Carl cupped her breast and gave it a squeeze.

"Carl," she said.

Carl gently unbuttoned her blouse and unhooked her bra. "Rena, you are so beautiful," he said looking at her breasts. His head moved down and he took her nipple in his mouth, licking, pulling gently, and softly caressing the other breast with his other hand. Rena moaned.

Carl gently pulled her to him and kissed her again. Rena felt her nipples harden even more and felt a throbbing between her legs. "Carl," she said moving to unbutton his jeans. She unbuttoned the top of his jeans and pulled the zipper down. She grabbed him and felt his erection between her hands. She caressed and stroked him gently. She could hear him moan and his breath become more ragged.

"Rena," he said moving her hand. "Wait," he said kissing her. He unbuttoned her jeans and pulled them down and off her legs. Her panties felt moist. He moved up on the bed, put his hand between her legs, and squeezed gently.

"Ooh," Rena said feeling the blood rush between her legs. Carl leaned down and kissed her panties. Then he slowly slid them down her legs, kissing the inside of her thighs and he moved down. "Oh my god, Carl," said she writhing. "Please," she begged wanting him to relieve her.

"Be patient," he said giving her a sly smile. He removed her panties from her ankles and kissed his way back up her body. His hand caressed her legs and buttocks as he moved back up. He kissed her lips between her legs and Rena thought she was going to go mad.

"Rena," he said moving up and kissing her on the mouth. He started kissing her neck and Rena could feel his fingers caress her vulva and find her clitoris. He fingers gently simulated the clitoris. Rena felt her body start to shake.

"Rena," Carl whispered into her ear and moved down to suck on her nipples. His breath was hot and Rena's nipples hardened instantly. She could feel him play with her clitoris and could feel the pressure starting to mount.

"Carl" she said grabbing at his jeans to pull them down.

Carl looked up and stared into her eyes. He removed his shirt and pants never taking his eyes off of her. He brought his hand back between her legs and gently squeezed. Rena moved her hands up and down his chest. Carl gently inserted his fingers inside Rena and started moving them. Rena writhed against his fingers and matched the movement of his fingers.

"Ohh," she moaned. She looked up to see Carl looking down at her. His body was gleaming with sweat and his erection was throbbing. Rena looked at his erection and could feel her body react.

"Rena, you are so damn beautiful," Carl said looking down at her.

"Oooh," Rena said feeling the pressure between her legs intensify.

With one swift movement, Carl removed his fingers and Rena felt him enter her. "Ohh," she said as Carl starting moving inside her. Rena moved with him, the ache between her legs begging for release. She could hear Carl's breath becoming more ragged and heard him moan. He started to move faster and Rena matched him moving her hips to rock with his. She could hear herself moaning and could hear Carl's moans match hers. The rocking intensified and Rena could hear the headboard bang against the wall, and hear the straining of the bedsprings.

"Oh, oh," cried Rena feeling like she was at the edge of a precipice. Her whole body ached for the release. "Don't stop, oh," she cried out as her body shuddered against his. She felt a surge of liquid between her legs and her whole body was bathed with pleasure. She heard him moan and move deeper into her, and then swiftly then heard him cry out and felt him release inside her.

He collapsed against her and Rena held onto him. She could feel his quick heart beat against hers as they both tried to catch their breath. Carl moved over a bit to the side and held Rena close to him. "I love you Rena," he said closing his eyes.

"I love you Carl," she said.

***

"Wake up sleepy head," she heard him say.

"Hmm," Rena said snuggling in closer. She could feel him kiss the top of her head.

"Rena," she heard him say. She sighed. She felt relaxed, comfortable, and snug. She didn't want to get up.

"Rena, I have to bring you to Anna's," he said, "I have to get to work."

Damn. She was hoping that she was dreaming and could still sleep. She slowly opened her eyes and looked into the deep brown eyes of her lover. "Hello my golden haired beauty," he said.

"Hello my dark-eyed stallion," she replied.

"What?" asked Carl breaking into laughter.

"I-I don't know," said Rena laughing with him. "I was trying to match your golden haired beauty comment," she said laughing.

Carl leaned over and kissed her soundly on the mouth. "Love you," he said.

She beamed. "Love you too," she said.

"Good," said Carl. "Now you have to get up, I have to go to work and Anna will kill me if I don't get you to her soon," he said.

"Are you afraid of her?" Rena teased.

"Yes," said Carl nodding his head in agreement.

Rena chuckled. "Okay then, let's go," she said slowly getting up.

CHAPTER 44

The guys moved passed Rena into the kitchen carrying the table. "Just put it down here," she said directing them. She moved over to continue unpacking the glasses. "I can't believe you lived with only three glasses!" she exclaimed.

"I only needed three," Carl said. "One for me, one for guests, and one extra just in case," he said grinning. He moved behind Rena and put his arms around her belly. "I just got kicked!" he exclaimed.

"Yup," said Rena, "You are getting kicked for only having three glasses!" she said giggling. She could feel Carl's breath on her neck. He kissed her lightly. She could feel his hands move down her belly to the sides of her hips. He moved them up and down her thighs on top and quickly on the inside. "Carl," she said admonishing him, but enjoying it at the same time.

"What's wrong?" he whispered seductively in her ear.

"Nothing, but... oooh," she said as his hands moved up and down her thighs again.

"I'm looking forward to christening the bedroom tonight," he said.

Rena turned to face him. "Umm Carl, we have already done that, many *many* times," she reminded him.

"Yes, but, this is the first time you will be all moved in," he said kissing her. "It's different," he said kissing her again and pulling her close to him.

"Yes, it is," she said wrapping her arms around this neck. "Are you all done painting the nursery?" she asked.

"Yes, well nearly," Carl said kissing her again and moving his hands to cup her buttocks. "I just had to see you," he said pressing her against the counter. His tongue teased her and Rena felt the heat rise in her body. She moved her arms from around his neck and slid them down his hips to grab his buttocks. "Rena," he said breathlessly moving his hands to her waist and pulling her closer to him.

"Whoa," said Falcone coming into the kitchen carrying a box. "You guys are like rabbits. This is what got you into trouble in the first place," he said putting the box on the counter grinning.

"I like this kind of trouble," Carl growled pulling Rena closer to him and kissing her soundly on the mouth. Rena giggled.

"Are you two still at it?" Anna exclaimed walking into the kitchen with another box.

"Yes, it's sickening, just sickening," joked Falcone shaking his head.

"How's my god child?" Anna asked moving Carl out of the way and touching Rena's tummy.

"Good, kicking up a storm," Rena said smiling.

"Oh, he just wants to see his Zia Anna," Anna said leaning into Anna's belly and talking.

"Yah, that's it," said Falcone rolling his eyes and laughing.

"Hey, it's true," said Anna getting annoyed.

"Okay, okay guys," Rena said. "My baby will love you both equally," she said giving Anna a hug. "Poor thing will be sleeping in a drawer though, as his daddy has not put his crib together yet," Rena said jokingly, looking at Carl.

Carl laughed. "Okay, I will go and do that now," he said giving Rena's belly a quick kiss.

"Like I said, rabbits," Falcone said winking at Rena as he followed Carl out of the kitchen.

Anna put her arms around her friend. "Rena, I am so happy for you," she said. "You are blossoming," she said beaming at her friend.

"Anna, I feel so lucky," Rena said. "I never thought I would have love again," she said.

Anna looked intently at her friend. "My Zia Teresa always told me that if you get a second chance at something you shouldn't waste it," Anna said, "that we shouldn't be afraid to start over, because it's a chance to make things better."

"I'm so lucky that I got the chance to start again," Rena said.

"Me too," said Carl walking into the room. He moved

over to Rena and looked deeply into her eyes. "Every morning with you is like starting again Rena. Every day is bigger and better than the day before."

Rena looked deeply into his eyes. She knew she was home. All of the past had washed away. Her memories of Jarod had faded, blinded by the love that she and Carl shared. She knew deeply in her heart, that there was nothing better than this. With Carl, she knew every day was a new beginning, and a new opportunity - to start again.

EPILOGUE

Rena's body ached all over. The pressure in her loins was intense. She could feel his bated breath; close to her ear; hear his moans. She felt sexy, glorious, and horny. She needed him now, inside her, desperately. The intensity of the feeling made her cry out and beg. "Please, oh please," she begged staring at his pulsating hardness.

She licked her lips. She wanted him; she *needed* him. She could feel the moistness between her legs contract in anticipation. "Pllleease," she begged, moving her hips closer to his.

His mouth crushed hers and she could feel his tongue, probing, licking, and sucking. He bit her lip, pulled, and sucked on it. She could feel the moistness between her legs pulsating. She needed him *now*.

He looked at her closely. "Look at me," he said as he entered her.

Her whole body felt a bathe of warmth as he entered her, moving back and forth, inside and out, rubbing against her. Her teeth tingled. "Oh my god," she said, feeling the urgency in her loins.

Her body started to shake beneath his and her hips urged him to move faster. He cupped her buttocks and moved deeper inside her. His movements intensified and he started to move faster, harder, penetrating her. Her body felt on fire and she could feel the heat emanating from his body. My god, she loved this man. He plunged even deeper inside her and she gasped at the feeling of pleasure. Her hips moved faster and he grabbed her buttocks tight to keep her moving with him. She could feel herself at the edge. She could feel his breath and his gasps for air as he moved expertly inside her. She could feel her softness and warm heat envelope him. He continued to kiss and tease her as he moved. She was going to die of pleasure. She gripped his shoulders tightly as she felt herself move to the precipice. He plunged in her one more time and her body shuddered in release. She cried out again and again in ecstasy. She felt him release inside her and hear his sounds of pleasure as his hot sweaty body fell on top of her. She could hear him trying to catch his breath and could feel the quick beating of his heart.

"Holy shit," he said.

"Holy cow," she said.

He laughed. "Holy cow," he said. He froze. His head moved up to listen. She listened as well. Nothing. He collapsed again upon her. She rubbed her hands up and down his back.

"I love you," she said kissing his neck.

"I love you baby," he said leaning up and kissing her. He froze again. "Oh," he said, giving her a quick kiss on the mouth and grinning.

"Enjoy," she said relaxing into the bed.

He looked at her. "Rena, God only gave me two hands," he said.

She sighed smiling. "I know, I know," she said and started to get up.

They sauntered naked into the nursery. "I'll take Matthew," he said leaning into the crib to pick up his son.

"I'll take Carl junior," she said picking up their little surprise.

They looked into each other's eyes; the love they shared was real, naked, like them. They moved together and kissed. The twins could wait for a minute.

ABOUT THE AUTHOR

Ann Kingsdale has always loved romance novels. After spending many years writing technical documentation, she decided to embrace her love of romance and write from her heart. Ann spends many hours wandering the woods near her home, daydreaming about new stories for her books. She lives just north of Toronto, Canada with her family and her beloved pooch.